FATHER

Tales from an I...

By Barbara Allen

Text Copyright 2023 © Barbara Allen.

All Rights Reserved.

With the exception of quotes used in reviews, this book may not be reproduced or used in whole or in part by any means existing without written permission from the aforementioned author.

Warning: The unauthorised reproduction or distribution of this copyrighted work is illegal. No part of this book may be scanned, uploaded or distributed via the Internet or any other means, electronic or print, without the author's written permission.

This book is a work of fiction and any resemblance to persons, living or dead is purely coincidental. The characters are productions of the author's imagination and used fictitiously.

CONTENTS

1. PUCKLORGLIN   Page 1

2. SAINT PATRICK'S DAY   Page 7

3. THE VISIT   Page 19

4. WALKING ON WATER   Page 33

5. EASTER   Page 43

6. IT'S THE LITTLE THINGS   Page 53

7. GABRIEL   Page 69

8. FATHER FORGIVE ME   Page 79

9. FATHER JOHN LOVES CHRISTMAS   Page 93

10. THE CHURCH HALL DISCO   Page 107

PUCKLORGLIN

As the bus swayed through the Kerry countryside, Father John felt happy to be leaving the city. Starting his new parish in the country town of Pucklorglin was just the challenge he needed. The warnings he'd been given, that he would be going back in time, didn't bother him. A country parish would be refreshing after the madness of Dublin.

Father John's only real concern was being the replacement for the newly departed, and much-loved, Father Frank. Who, after a night in O'Shea's pub, had tripped over a grassy verge by the road, and fallen into an inebriated sleep.

Peter McAlarney, who was also on his way home from the pub that fateful day, had tried with difficulty to steer his bike around Father Frank's head, as it lay peacefully on the edge of the road, but failed and ploughed straight over it instead. When asked by the judge why he didn't stop, Peter McAlarney said that he was too drunk to get off his bike and help him.

After great deliberation, the judge's verdict was accidental death by dangerously riding a bicycle under the influence of alcohol.

Peter McAlarney gave his bike to charity and took the pledge never to drink again.

When Father John was told of the tragedy, he couldn't believe his ears.

Father John Phelan was six foot two inches tall, with a fine head of black wavy hair, and a beautiful tenor voice that could charm a banshee on a stormy night. In his youth, he played rugby, and boxed for his college, attaining the nickname, 'The Shillelagh.' It was as much of a shock to himself as to others when he decided to join the priesthood.

When asked why he took holy orders, 'Who knows what the man upstairs has in store for you?' was his answer.

He was a quiet man, finding that others did all the talking. But he didn't suffer fools lightly, and on many occasions, his was the last word.

Father John was jolted from his thoughts by the bus driver calling out, 'Next stop, Little Pucklorglin.'

'Pucklorglin, did you say?'

'That's right, Father, sure it is.' The driver pulled the bus to a halt.

Struggling with his suitcase, Father John stepped from the bus onto a thin pavement in front of a rickety wooden bus shelter. Looking around him, he wondered which direction to take for the church. Opposite the bus stop, a man was watching him from his garden.

'Top of the morning, Father. Can I help in any way?'

'I'm looking for the church. I'm the new parish priest now that Father Frank is no longer with us, God rest his soul.'

'Father Frank from Pucklorglin you're talking about? Well now, this is Little Pucklorglin you're in. You'll be wanting the bus for Pucklorglin.'

Confused, Father John said, 'The bus driver told me this was Pucklorglin.'

'In a manner of speaking, so it is.' The man stood up straight, clearing his throat as he got ready to impart his superior knowledge. 'As I said, you're in Little Pucklorglin. The next stop is Middle Pucklorglin. You don't need either of these for the church, that's in Pucklorglin. If you hurry you can catch the bus.' He pointed to the same one that Father John had arrived on, which was still loitering at the bus stop.

Thinking the man was joshing, Father John started to laugh, but the man's expression remained serious. 'This really isn't Pucklorglin?'

'No, Father.'

'Well, thank you for your help. I look forward to seeing you at Mass on Sunday.'

'No, Father, that's not my religion. I'm not Catholic. I'm a naturist.'

'A naturist? Since when was that a religion, then?'

'If it was good enough for Adam and Eve, it's good enough for me, Father.'

Father John didn't argue with the man's biblical knowledge. Giving him a priestly smile of acknowledgement, he thanked him for the directions, and headed back to the bus.

'Hello again, Father.' The bus driver was surprised to see him. 'That was a quick visit, so it was. Where is it to this time?'

'Pucklorglin. I'm the new parish priest.'

'Pucklorglin? Why didn't you say that in the first place? There's no church here.'

'I noticed. Now tell me, is this the bus I'm needing?'

'In a manner of ways, it is.'

Puzzled, Father John asked, 'What manner would that be then?'

'Well now, I'll be telling you. This bus is shared by three companies. One bus to Little Pucklorglin, one bus to Middle Pucklorglin, and one bus to Pucklorglin.'

'But it's the same bus!'

'I agree that's how it seems. I work for all three companies, and each has a different bus stop. So, if it's Pucklorglin you want, that's the correct stop ahead of you. This one is for Middle Pucklorglin, and the one behind—'

'Is for Little Pucklorglin?'

'Correct, Father. You catch on fast. Most people find it complicated.'

He raised his eyes to heaven. *Holy mother of God, am I dreaming this?* 'Do you mean to tell me, if I get on this bus again, it will take me to Pucklorglin?'

'It will, Father, but it will cost you more to go to the next stop, as technically speaking you're getting on another bus owned by a different company.'

Looking at the bus driver, Father John wondered if a degree in geography was needed to get to his destination. 'I don't care how much, which bus, which company. Just give me a ticket to Pucklorglin.'

'I understand your frustration, Father. But the more you travel on the bus, the more it will be as clear as the day is long.'

Father John handed over the ticket money, only to be stopped by a drawn out 'Ah' from the driver. 'I've just realised it's Thursday. This bus company doesn't go to Pucklorglin on Thursday, only as far as Middle Pucklorglin. So I can't legally accept your fare. You have to go to the other stop for Pucklorglin.'

Playing along with the driver, he asked, 'At what time does the other bus go to Pucklorglin?'

'Midday. You have plenty of time.'

'Wouldn't it be easier if I stayed on this bus?'

'You can, of course, but, as I said, I will have to charge you for one stop extra.'

'So be it then.' Father John handed over the extra ticket money, took his seat, and watched the hands of his watch until they met on the appointed hour for departure. The comforting hum of the bus engine starting up was music to his ears.

'How far from the bus stop to the church?' he asked the driver.

'The bus stop? Now let me think, it's been a while since I stopped there. Better I drop you off at the top of the village. It's not too far to walk from there.'

'You have a long drive back. I don't want to put you out in any way.'

'You're not, Father. I live opposite the church, and the bus company has an arrangement with Bishop Kelly to park the bus in the church's car park overnight.'

It had been a long day, and another minute discussing the running of the bus companies was more than any sane man could listen to.

'Would you like me to drop you off at the church? It's a long walk to carry a heavy suitcase, so it is.'

Holy mother of God and all the saints in heaven, give me patience. Father John thanked the driver, wondering if with his new parish he had slipped into a parallel universe.

Bidding the driver goodnight, and refusing a drink at O'Shea's pub, he made his way to the presbytery. With hope and anticipation in his heart, he knocked on the door, wondering what lay ahead.

SAINT PATRICK'S DAY

Kathleen Byrne, housekeeper at the presbytery of Saint Jude the Obscure, was a small, wiry woman with striking red hair that could almost glow in the dark. "Hard work," her mother had told her, "is the gateway to heaven."

Kathleen had lost count of the number of times her mother had said, "Try and emulate the nun that had to get on her knees to scrub the floor. Even though her knees were ulcerated, she never complained, poor woman." Who this suffering nun was, Kathleen never found out, but her suffering laid the foundation for a strong work ethic. Her reward for following her mother's sacred text was reading the Kerryman newspaper, accompanied by a small glass of Guinness at the end of the day.

Kathleen was chairwoman of the Catholic Women's League, which she ran with a determination that warranted a sainthood. Jumble sales, summer fetes and feast days—all fell under her watchful eye. What she didn't know about the people in Pucklorglin never stayed that way for long. She was a great asset to the church. It hadn't taken Father John long to realise that he would find it difficult to run any church events without her.

Looking at the calendar, Father John could hardly believe it was six weeks since he arrived in Pucklorglin. One wedding and six funerals ago. Not to mention the never to be forgotten episode when Jerry Keogh made a nuisance of himself by waking half the village trying to open his neighbour's front doors after closing time at

O'Shea's Pub.

The Boyles' wedding in particular was a touch and go affair; the uncertainty being due to whether there would be a christening on the same day. Thankfully for the warring families of the bride and groom, the wedding went ahead as planned. And the christening was all arranged for March the seventeenth, Saint Patrick's Day.

Father John was looking forward to the saint's day celebrations. However, the condition of the saint's statue was an embarrassment to the parish. And he wasn't the only one who despaired of its sorry state. Kathleen had felt the same from the first day she'd set eyes on it—for its cloak wasn't green, but blue.

'Right, Father,' Kathleen thrust the paintbrush into his hand, 'let's get started. Up the ladder you go. I'll steady it for you.'

Marvelling at Kathleen's determination in getting things done, Father John did as he was told, and soon found himself staring into the eyes of Saint Patrick. 'Well now, Paddy me boy,' he said affectionately, 'this won't do at all, at all. It's a miracle we'll be needing to get you ready for your big day, let alone a pot of paint.'

Kathleen clung onto the ladder as she clicked her tongue in disapproval. 'Whoever heard of Saint Patrick with a blue cloak? Sure, wouldn't Jaysus himself cry at the colour?'

'Well, at least it was that way before I came to the parish. Why in God's name did Father Frank buy your man with a blue cloak in the first place?'

'Sure, it wasn't his fault, God rest his soul. It was a visiting priest from China. He had a brother that made statues of your

Buddha fellow, and Confusion, and those stone dogs you see on holiday brochures.'

'Confusion? You mean Confucius, Kathleen.'

'That's right, Father, you have it to a tee. Exactly the same, but different. Anyway, his brother didn't have a statue of Saint Patrick, so he was sent a holy picture of him to copy. When the statue arrived, Father Frank was so relieved that the statue didn't have the same ears as your Buddha, that he said nothing about the colour of the cloak.'

'I would have sent it back and asked for a refund. The church is not made of money.'

'He couldn't, sure it was a gift.'

Father John dipped the brush into the paint, knowing there was no hope of buying a replacement statue in time, for Saint Patrick's feast day. The Sunday collection had more pressing demands, and Bishop Kelly, never a generous man, had told him in no uncertain terms that the diocese could not help.

Steadying his hand, he started to paint the front neckline of the cloak. As he did so, he tried to advert his gaze from the poor state of the previous putty repair on Saint Patrick's nose. A repair that deprived the snake charmer of Ireland of ever smelling the turf fires again.

Suddenly the church doors opened with an almighty crash. Kathleen jumped in fright, causing the ladder to wobble, and caused Father John's paintbrush to shoot upwards across the statue's face, and sploshing itself right across one of its eyes.

Father John had no sooner regained his balance, when thundering footsteps echoed down the aisle as Maggi O'Leary propelled herself towards them.

'Have you lost your senses, woman, not to mention your respect for this church?' Father John growled as he got down from the ladder.

'Respect you call it, Father, when you have agreed to baptise my grandson with a name like Wyatt Earp. He's an Irish catholic, not an American cowboy. If you go through with it, I'll change my religion to one of those, those…' she gulped over her words, 'those… foreign ones.'

'It's not surprising they chose that name,' retorted Father John. 'After all, wasn't it a shotgun wedding?'

'That's as may be, Father, but in the name of decency can't you talk to them? My daughter should never have married that culshie, even though she had to, what with the baby and all. Now he's trying to impress his American uncle, the eejit. The man's never been to Ireland, then writes to say that he's coming over for a slice of the old country, and he'd appreciate the christening be held on Saint Patrick's Day. I'll give him the old country when I see him.'

'Your temper will be the death of you, Maggi O'Leary. Have you forgotten the wedding, when you aimed your handbag at your son-in-law, and it hit Saint Patrick's nose? Now look at what you made me do to him today by storming in here.'

Taking a deep breath, Father John turned to his companion. 'Kathleen, will you be going to put the kettle on? Do take Mrs

O'Leary into the parlour. I'll join you both in a minute, then we can discuss everything in a civilised manner.'

Relieved to have five minutes' peace, Father John knew he had a problem. The O'Leary family on the one hand, and the Boyles on the other. At least, to everyone's relief, the death threats had stopped when Jimmy Boyle, who was quite a lad, not only agreed to marry Maggi O'Leary's daughter, but did so before the christening.

On the day of the wedding, every family in the village had turned out. Half to see the groom finally tamed. The other to see the size of the bride.

Father John started back up the ladder, only to see that the paint mark on Saint Patrick's face made him look like Sitting Bull. Trying to remove the paint made things worse. If a new statue of Saint Patrick hadn't been needed before, it was certainly needed now. But how to get one? Steadying himself down the ladder, Father John walked to the altar and knelt. The only thing to do was to talk to the man upstairs.

'Dear God, I need some help,' he began, 'can you tell me, what horse is certain to win at the races tomorrow?'

A few minutes later, silently avoiding the parlour, and the voice of Maggi O'Leary bemoaning her daughter's fate, he quickly headed to his office to phone Kevin Brady, the local turf accountant.

'Is that you, Mr Brady?' he whispered, trying to disguise his voice.

'It is, Father. What can I do for you?'

His cover blown, he continued, 'Have you got a good tip for tomorrow's race? It must be a certainty, though.'

'Nothing in life is a certainty, you know that, Father. What about Sitting Bull in the 3:30? It's two hundred to one. If you win, you're a lucky man.'

Father John was struck dumb. 'Did you say Sitting Bull?'

'I did. How much do you want to put on?'

After regaining his voice, he said, 'A pound to win. That will give me £200, right?'

'Correct. A pound and a prayer it is then.'

Replacing the receiver, Father John was now full of faith and expectation. Faith at the horse being called Sitting Bull. And the expectation of winning two hundred pounds could not be ignored. Even so, being a practical man, he decided to buy pink paint for the statue's face, just in case.

'There, there, Mrs O'Leary, take a sip of tea. It's hot and sweet and will do you a power of good,' Kathleen said sympathetically. 'The Father will try to sort everything out. So don't go worrying yourself in advance. Do you hear me?'

'I'm sure you're right, Mrs Byrne, and I'm sorry for being a nuisance. But nobody would call a child Wyatt Earp now, would they?'

Kathleen was about to say that her son-in-law *was* a strange exception, but thankfully was stopped in time by Father John coming into the parlour.

Looking at Father John, Kathleen thought that if she didn't know better, she would have said he had a smug look on his face.

Maggi O'Leary, only half pacified about her grandson's christening name, finally left. Father John knew her rantings and ravings wouldn't solve her problem. Only a miracle could sort everything out. This was turning out to be a game of cowboys and Indians in more ways than one.

The following day, Father John painted Saint Patrick's face pink. Staring at the statue's newly painted complexion reminded him of a bag of marshmallows. *Holy mother of God, what are we to do?*

The voice of Kevin Brady gave him a jolt. 'I was passing, so I thought I would pop in. Your horse Sitting Bull has been withdrawn from the race.'

'Withdrawn, did you say?'

'He was, Father. So, I put your pound on a real outsider, five hundred to one—and he was first past the post! It was a miracle to say the least. Good day for you, bad day for me. What are you going to do with the winnings? More work on the church roof?'

Before Father John had time to reply, Kevin Brady took a step backwards. 'Jaysus, what's that?' He pointed to the statue's face. 'Has Maggi O'Leary been at him again? Which reminds me, the horse that won was called Paddy's Mantle.'

Father John was near speechless at the horse's name. 'Paddy's Mantle?' he repeated, blessing himself. 'God works in mysterious ways, that's for sure.'

'You can say that again.' Kevin stared up at the bright-pink-painted face. 'If I was you, Father, I would be inclined to buy a new statue.'

As a smirking Kevin left, Father John looked at Saint Patrick's sad, pink face, and the one emerald green eye that stared at him, and momentarily felt sad. 'I'm sorry to say it's time for you to go. Make way for the new, you understand.' Jumping down from the ladder, and respectively making the sign of the cross, he all but ran down the aisle heading for his office, his winnings burning a hole in his pocket.

Within five minutes a new statue was ordered, this time from Dublin. With a cloak of glorious green, and a matching mitre. The base looked as if it was almost alive with writhing snakes. Then, to top it all, a halo of sparkling light bulbs adorned the figure. Father John was elated. *Now there's only the shootout at the O.K. Corral to worry about.*

The Saint Patrick's Day service was a great success. The church lights were dimmed to show off the sparkling halo on the new statue. Shamrock was proudly pinned to every dress and lapel. The singing echoed in every corner, as the congregation, led by Father John, were in full voice, singing to "Glorious Saint Patrick, Dear Saint Of Our Isle."

Then it was time for the christening.

Silence descended in the church. Not out of respect for the

christening to take place, but not wanting to miss any altercations between the warring families.

Father John waited till everyone was assembled around the baptismal font. The stony look on Maggi O'Leary's face had the power to turn the holy water to ice. For try as he might, a solution to change the name could not be found.

'Today is a special day for the two families here present,' began Father John. 'Especially for the proud parents of the youngest member.'

Maggi O'Leary fidgeted with her handbag, as she passed it from one arm to the other.

Father John continued, keeping his eye on her familiar weapon of choice.

'This day,' he emphasised, 'is not about names. It's about welcoming this child to our church. Let us each,' looking at Maggi O'Leary, 'reflect on this with a silent prayer.' *Well now, this is my last chance, or Wyatt Earp it will be. You know I tried talking to them, but neither side would change their mind.* Looking up, Father John blessed himself. 'Now pass the child to me.'

Father John held the baby as he scooped the holy water into the little silver cup. He paused; the name Wyatt Earp was on the tip of his tongue, but refused to come. The baby started to cry, which set off the warring families. At the same time, the sparkling bulbs on the saint's halo started to flash. There was no choice, Wyatt Earp it had to be. The silver cup of water trembled in his hand as he got ready to wet the baby's head. Just as he was about to speak, there was an abrupt tugging on his mantle. It was Jimmy Boyle's little sister.

'Fader, fader,' she said, pointing to Saint Patrick's flashing halo lights. 'What's his name?'

How the next thing happened was the miracle he prayed for. At the same time as he was going to say Wyatt Earp, he looked to the statue, then to the child. 'Patrick,' he said, as he poured the water on the baby's head.

'Patrick Wyatt Earp, I baptise you in the name of the Father and of the Son, and of the Holy Ghost. Amen.'

The lull before the storm didn't last long. But when it came, it was an eruption of laughter from both sides of the family. Maggi O'Leary laughed so much she cried. This compelled Mrs Boyle Senior to put her arm around her. The warring fathers shook hands, the congregation cheered, the baby screamed, and Father John sang the closing hymn solo, his grand voice filling the church.

Before joining the christening party at William O'Shea's pub, Father John sat down in a quiet corner of the church.

'Dear God, peace at last.' Making the sign of the cross, he continued, 'I'll tell you something, Lord. Paddy's Mantle coming in first was the best pound I have ever spent, and didn't Saint Patrick's halo save the day? No matter if you tried, you couldn't make it up.' "Patrick Wyatt Earp"—just saying the name made him laugh. 'Anyways, thank you for a grand day. In the name of the Father, the Son, and the Holy Ghost, Amen.'

The party at William O'Shea's pub afterwards resulted in a lot of sorry heads. The following day, Jimmy Boyle's uncle returned to America, with all the expectations of the old country satisfied. But still completely perplexed why anyone would have wanted to call a baby Wyatt Earp in the first place.

THE VISIT

Father John was up early. He loved the peace of the mornings with just the birdsong for company. And then to start his day with a chat to the man upstairs.

Lighting a candle to Saint Patrick first, he thanked the saint for the successful outcome at the christening. The thought of what Bishop Kelly would have said about a new Catholic given the name Wyatt Earp might have seen him shipped out to do missionary work with a newly discovered tribe in the Amazon.

After genuflecting in front of the altar, Father John sat down on one of the pews. 'Dear God, now wasn't that a successful outcome. Two families reunited, a new statue, and a baby with a good Irish name. Let us pray that Bishop Akuma from Africa will enjoy his visit to Pucklorglin. Which brings me to an idea I have for the church…'

Back in the presbytery, Father John felt that he had explained his idea to the man upstairs clearly, but unusually, he had come away from the church without any guidance from the Almighty. Looking hopefully at Kathleen, he tapped a finger on a picture in the brochure spread open before them. 'Well, what about this one?'

'You can show them all to me, I don't like your idea. Where in God's name do you get them from? Sure, we're a church, not a bingo hall. Trying to impress the African bishop with flashing lights saying, "Jesus leads the way", or "God is our guide", will leave him thinking we have money to burn. What would he think of that, when his own congregation's collection box is frequently half empty. No Father, millionaires we are not. And while we're on the subject of money, what about finding some funds to get Jerry Keogh his guide dog? Sure, half the village are being deprived of sleep with him losing his way.'

Father John sat stony faced. He'd never mentioned money and was perplexed about Jerry Keogh's guide dog.

Kathleen continued, 'All this electrical technical stuff is far removed from lions and drought.'

'What in God's name are you talking about, woman? The bishop comes from modern Africa, with running water, and cats for pets. Not the time of the Zulu wars. God forgive me Kathleen, but sometimes…'

'And sometimes to you too, Father. But, if you're that set, and you think light bulbs will make a difference to our Lord's words, well carry on, so.'

A dilemma had arisen. *To light up, or not to light up.* Later, after some serious thought, Father John decided Kathleen was right. The entertainment budget from the diocese for the visiting bishop was small, and the list of things to arrange was long. They didn't need to waste money on fancy lights.

One request was for traditional Irish village entertainment, before television and the internet took over. Father John thought that a strange request, but if that was what Bishop Kelly wanted, he had to do it.

It was a short walk to Flynn McCoul's house. He was the only man Father John could think of who was old enough to remember how the villagers entertained themselves in the old days.

Father John knocked on the green gloss front door, but to no avail. He tried again with more force. Flynn was 94, and his wife, Hannah, nearly the same age, so, he concluded, they were probably a little deaf. He continued knocking until he heard footsteps in the hall, and the front door opened.

'Hello, Flynn,' shouted Father John, 'can you spare us a minute?'

'No need to shout, Father, I'm not deaf.'

'Did you not hear me knocking on the door?'

'I did, of course, why else would I have opened it?'

There wasn't a quick answer to that. 'Are you busy, Flynn? I have a few questions to ask you about years gone by in the village.'

'Busy or no, come in and ask away. My wife's inside, she'll tell you all you want to know. Wasn't she blessed as a child with the memory of the little people.'

Father John settled himself down, as Hannah told him of days of fun and laughter. 'It wasn't all sunshine and roses though, Father, things could be hard. But we always had the Saturday night dance at the village hall to look forward to.' Hannah sighed. 'That's where I met your man here.' She pointed at Flynn. 'He was the best dancer in the village, so he was.'

'A village dance, you say. Well thank you, Hannah. You have solved my problem. That's what we'll have for the African bishop's visit—a village dance. Tell me, how many were in the band?'

'What band would that be, Father?'

'The band for the dance.'

'Oh, we didn't have a band,' interrupted Flynn. 'Just a—'

'Ah, just a fiddle player, was it?'

'Far from fiddle players we were born, Father. The nearest was miles away, and he refused to walk here again. Sure, the old fellow didn't have any shoes.'

'Mother of God, no shoes, did you say?'

'That's right, Father. Took his boots off the last time he came here, on account of his blisters,' Flynn closed his eyes in remembrance, 'and the next morning they were gone.'

'He should have left them somewhere safe.'

'Oh, he did that now. In the church porch. None of your electrical light in those days. We all knew who took them, though. It was a young gosson, Billy Boreen. The boy never had shoes on his feet before, and you could hear him coming, as the boots were two sizes too big for him. Mind you, Father, in one respect the fiddle player had his revenge. A horse and cart went over Billy's foot at the cattle fair, and he had always to buy two pairs of shoes for the rest of his life.'

'Two pairs of shoes?' asked Father John, slightly perplexed.

'One shoe two sizes too big on account of the injury, and the other—'

The conversation brought back memories of his first day on the Pucklorglin bus and the baffling conversation he'd had with the driver. This time, he decided not to ask any questions.

Flynn continued, 'There was another young gossone who played the spoons. We had a grand sound from them. He disappeared after the funeral, and we never saw him again.'

'Holy mother in heaven, Flynn.' His wife, exasperated, shook her head. 'Wasn't it his own funeral, God rest his soul. Terrible to see his mother bereaved of her only son.'

Father John blessed himself. 'An only child, was he?'

'He was so, Father, apart from his fifteen sisters.'

By now, Father John wondered if he had arrived in a mad house. Missing boots, crushed feet, and an only child with fifteen sisters. He was beginning to think he'd never get this dance off the floor.

'Flynn, if it wasn't a band, a fiddle player, or the spoons, what in God's name did accompany you at the dance?'

Throwing back his head, Flynn laughed so hard even his wife thought his remaining three teeth would slip down his throat and choke him. 'Show him, Hannah,' he spluttered. 'Bands and fiddles? Here in the middle of nowhere? Sure, not many people knew we were here at all.'

Hannah shuffled across the flagstone floor and stood in front of them. Then, in a voice that sounded like the wail of a banshee, the first 'diddley, diddley, darly, darly' sprang from her lips and bounced off the cottage walls. Flynn, motivated by past memories, stood up, clapping his hands to the rhythm, before taking his wife into his arms and spinning her around in circles.

Father John sat, open mouthed, hoping to God that neither of them would have a heart attack.

Hannah, out of breath, finally stopped. 'That brought back happy memories, Father. I hope when I get old, I won't forget the steps. They were the best dances I ever went to.'

Father John was impressed at Hannah's idea of old age.

'We danced all night to the mouth music,' said Flynn. 'Not forgetting to keep the boyo's throat lubricated with good Irish whiskey, so we did. Let me think now, what was his name?'

Father John nodded in amazement. *Jesus, Mary and Joseph. A diddly dar singer. If it's not the Amazon I'll be sent to, it will be to the ends of the earth after this African visit, to find the lost tribe of Israel, and convert them to Christianity.*

'Flynn,' prodded Hannah, 'was it not old Patrick Keogh who did the mouth music?'

'It was indeed. A real musical family. Even his great grandson has the gift.'

After listening to a rundown of the Keoghs' family tree, which felt as though it started with Adam and Eve, Flynn finally told Father John that the very man he wanted lived next door.

'You could have said that in the first place.'

To which Flynn replied, that he could, if he'd a mind to.

*

Jerry Keogh, to Father John's relief, was at home. Confirming what Flynn had told him, Jerry agreed to do the mouth music for the African bishop's visit.

'Good man yourself, Jerry. I'll say a prayer to Saint Celia for you tonight.'

'Better a prayer to Saint Francis for a donation towards a guide dog. That would suit me better.'

'You never said your eyes were failing you.'

'Why would I? My eyes are fine.'

'Then what in God's name do you need a guide dog for?'

'To guide me home. Sure, didn't I nearly catch my death from walking around looking for my house after closing time at O'Shea's.'

With the list of things he still had to do, Father John's patience was stretched to the limit. Speaking from the side of his mouth helped to control his frustration. 'Have you tried abstinence, Jerry?'

'I'm glad you brought that up, Father. I'll be coming to Mass this Sunday, so I will.'

Puzzled, Father John asked, 'What has that got to do with giving up drinking?'

'Who said anything about giving up drinking?'

Today was not the day to venture down a pointless alley of conversation. Taking his leave of Jerry Keogh, he headed back to the presbytery to make a start on the list of things he had to do before Bishop Akuma's visit.

During his absence, Kathleen had been busy phoning the members of the Catholic Women's League, asking each member if they were happy to help with arranging the catering for their special visitor. That done, the next job was to phone the scout master to get the boys to arrange the tables and chairs. Then the girl guides to make the welcome banners.

When Father John arrived back at the presbytery, he was relieved with all Kathleen had organized. 'Thank you, Kathleen. That's another couple of ticks on the pre-bishop's visit list. Also, my visit to Flynn and Hannah was well worth the time I spent with them. Bishop Kelly will be pleased, as they gave me the idea for the entertainment for Bishop Akuma's visit. It will be a traditional village dance. The music… well, I say music, its mouth music, and who do you think will be doing it?'

'Jerry Keogh, Father. His family were famous for it.'

'You could have told me, Kathleen. My head's in a spin, what with listening to Hannah's rendition and watching the two of them dancing a Kerry Reel. They spun so fast, it's amazing they didn't drill into the floor.'

Kathleen gave him a craggy stare. 'You should count yourself lucky you can at least see them. Not like poor Jerry Keogh, who needs that guide dog.'

Father John thought there was no point in telling her what the guide dog was for. Better that she found out for herself. That would be much more fun.

*

The day for the African bishop's visit had arrived. The final touches to the church hall were finished, and the tea urn was heating up nicely. The welcoming parishioners were giving themselves a final once over by brushing half the bogs of Ireland from their Sunday best, and licking down troublesome quiffs of hair that were determined to go their own way.

Kathleen went early to the hall to put cloths and flowers on the little tables, hiding the marks from years of continual use. The plates of food were arranged, and the bottle of whiskey purchased to lubricate Jerry Keogh's throat was put in a safe place. There was only one problem; her feet were killing her. *Sacred heart of Jaysus, what made me wear new shoes. My toes feel as though they're in a vice, and my heels are as raw as meat.*

Then she heard her mother's voice telling her about the nun with the ulcerated knees. *Holy mother of God. That one's knees will be the death of me.*

'Well, Kathleen,' said Father John. 'You have done us proud. The spread looks grand. Plenty to eat for everyone, and the flowers are the perfect finishing touch. All down to you, and the Catholic Women's League. Sure, you're a treasure, so you are.'

Fidgeting from foot to foot, she replied, 'Holy mother of God, I can't stand this any longer.'

Thinking it was something he said, Father John stood to attention. 'What can't you stand?'

'My feet, they're killing me. It's these new shoes, I'll have to take them off.'

'Why didn't you buy a sensible pair of lace ups, instead of those flipperty-gibbet things you're wearing?'

Kathleen gave Father John a stare that reminded him of a diving hawk heading towards its prey. It was only the arrival of Jerry Keogh and an emaciated dog which stopped Kathleen's reply.

'What in the name of God is that?' Father John circled the dog. 'You can't tell its head from its—'

'I found it on my doorstep, and it refused to leave. You could say he was heaven sent. This dog could be blindfolded, Father, and it would find its way back to my house. Just the guide dog I was looking for.'

Studying the dog, which was as thin as the Catholic Herald Newspaper, Father John could notice nothing of the guiding spirit about it, as it wandered towards a table.

'Heaven sent, it is that, Jerry,' Kathleen enthused. 'Now with the guide dog, and getting a medical opinion on your eyes, you might only need a pair of glasses.'

Jerry wondered why he needed a medical opinion on his eyes. 'A pair of glasses, Mrs Byrne?'

'Foggy vision comes to us all in time, Jerry. There's nothing to worry about. A good optician could sort that out for you. Does the dog have a name?'

'Doorstep, on account of—'

Before Jerry could continue, someone called out that a black car was pulling up outside. Kathleen bent down to retrieve her shoes, just as Jerry realised his dog had slipped its lead. Father John and Jerry both spotted the dog at the same time, lying under a table, chewing one of Kathleen's new shoes.

'Jaysus, I'm banjacked now, Father,' said Jerry, as he rushed out of sight.

Kathleen was introduced to their African guest, who, bemused at her stocking feet, smiled at her, nodding an understanding as she explained her situation.

'Excuse my feet, your Grace, the dog ruined one of my shoes.'

'There's nothing to excuse. People will look into your eyes to see the true you. Not at your feet.'

Sacred heart of Jaysus, he thinks I can't afford a pair of shoes. The shame of it. 'Oh no, your Grace, it was that dog.' She pointed.

The bishop looked at the empty space, nodding kindly. Father John, seeing the situation going from bad to worse from Kathleen's point of view, light-heartedly intervened on her behalf.

'There's nothing to be ashamed of, Kathleen. As his Grace said, nobody judges you by your feet.'

Father John, realising that his comment didn't help, moved on quickly, presenting Jerry Keogh to Bishop Akuma.

'This is Jerry, our music man for the dancing tonight. The same music that his great grandfather used to accompany the dances in his day. Bishop Kelly tells me you're interested in the traditional way things were done. Hopefully you won't be disappointed.'

'Tradition must be kept alive for future generations,' the bishop answered with concern. 'This modern world has me worried. Tradition to the young today is what happened yesterday. They are always looking to the next new craze, no matter how strange it is.'

'Strange is what they like, is it?' Father John said, thinking about the mouth music. 'Well, we will be sending you back with a strange new craze, that's for sure, I'll guarantee you that.'

Jerry Keogh began the evening in full vocal flourish with the first diddly, diddly notes of a Kerry Reel. Father John found it hard to relax as he watched Jerry's throat being lubricated, as per tradition, with good Irish whiskey. As for the dancing, you would have thought the floor in the old church hall would give way, with all the spinning and turning to the mouth music.

Bishop Akuma joined in, doing the Kerry Reel with distinctively African movements, which were copied by all. Kathleen, in only her stocking feet, allowed Bishop Akuma to swing her around to Jerry's surprisingly rhythmic mouth music.

'Thank you, dear lady.' Bishop Akuma bowed to Kathleen. 'I hope your feet are still in one piece. Even as a boy, I could never let such good music go to waste.'

As the evening drew to a close, not a crumb was left from the food and the tea urn had been exhausted, leaving them with William O'Shea's crates of Porta to give vent to many a toast. Both Irish, and African.

Kathleen then presented Bishop Akuma with an Aran cardigan, knitted by the Catholic Women's League. 'If you unravel a jumper,' she told him, 'it will tell you more about the person who knitted it, than the pattern you see.' This remark left the bishop wondering if the jumper was a garment to be worn or a traditional Irish puzzle to be solved.

'Dear people of Pucklorglin, thank you. Thank you for everything you have done to make me welcome. When I return to Africa, part of me will still feel a little Irish. Especially when I teach the ladies of my church the Kerry Reel.'

Father John rounded off the evening with a rendition of Danny Boy. Accompanied, not by Jerry Keogh, but by the howls of his new dog, Doorstep.

What a success the whole evening had been. Bishop Akuma wanted Jerry Keogh to visit him in Africa and teach him the mouth music. Jerry politely refused, saying that he could not on account of his new guide dog.

Father John's imagined threat of being sent to far flung places was now forgotten. As always, his faith intact, he decided to take a stroll to the church to have a chat with the man upstairs. Making it the perfect ending to a perfect day.

A month later, a large crate from Africa arrived, containing a neon sign saying, "Jesus Shows the Way." Bishop Akuma had included a note saying that he thought this would help people to find the church in the dark. Another parcel was also in the box. A gift of handwoven sandals for the poor lady with no shoes.

A smile crossed Father John's face. 'Oh, the days of the Kerry dances, oh, the hum of the piper's tune,' he sang as he hurried to phone the electrician.

WALKING ON WATER

Kathleen was thrilled to bits with her new sandals. 'They're so comfortable, Father, you would have thought they were made for me.'

'As I always say, Kathleen, God works in mysterious ways. Just look at Jerry Keogh, a reformed man since that thing of a dog turned up. And whatever made Bishop Akuma think that his gift of an electrical sign for the church was just what I wanted?'

Kathleen's only reply was to mutter her disapproval of neon signs. Father John let the subject drop, hoping she would come round to the sign when it was up and working. In the meantime, he had the weather to worry about.

Days of torrential rain were making Pucklorglin a soggy mess. Not only that, but the rain had found its way through the church roof—a recurring problem that needed facing sooner rather than later. Buckets and bowls littered the church aisles, which echoed with the sound of drips and splashes.

As if that wasn't enough, the stream that bordered Saint Jude's boundary had broken its banks and flooded the surrounding land.

Father John decided not to go cap in hand to the man upstairs for help with the church roof. He prayed for fine weather instead.

'Try to look on the bright side, Father, it will make the roses bloom.'

'You could be right, Kathleen, but with Jerry Keogh being

the new church gardener, I'm not convinced that he can tell the difference between a rose and a weed. All we'll be famous for will be our display of dandelions.'

'The garden's the least of your worries, Father. We had better start praying for dry weather in time for the folk music festival, as it's nearly upon us. We could get a good crowd here for that, which will boost the church funds towards the roof repairs. Mary from the shop rang to say she saw a convoy of travellers' vans arriving this morning, and they had posters on the side of them advertising the concert.'

'Posters on their vans, you say? That is good news. Let's hope the rain stops, and the posters stay put.' Being told this, a glimmer of light shone on the situation. 'Good weather will bring in a good crowd, and they might be in a giving mood if they visit Saint Jude's. I'll pop over to the church and sort out a few more collection boxes for the roof fund, just in case.'

While Father John was peacefully sorting through the boxes, the pleasing hush in the church was abruptly broken by the sound of snoring echoing from the confessional. Crossing the church at speed, Father John opened the door to find a white-faced, long-haired youth, who, if it weren't for the noise he was making, you would have thought had departed from this world.

'Holy mother of God,' he exclaimed, talking to himself, 'I'll have to get this fella awake and away.' He shook the youth by the shoulders. 'Come on, fella me lad, time to go home.'

Through the long hair that covered his face, one blurry eye

opened, then closed again.

Now what do I do? This fellow won't know it's today until tomorrow is over.

Before he had time to think, Jerry Keogh, covered in mud, burst into the church and ran up the aisle shouting, 'A dead body! A real dead body!'

Concentrating on the sleeping stranger, Father John said, 'He's not dead, he's resting.'

'Resting, you say? Thanks be to God, he's a lucky man,' said Jerry, blessing himself.

'What are you blessing yourself for, you eejit? I said he's not dead.'

'I heard you, Father. You said resting.'

'Who's at rest? Your man here is not dead. He's asleep.' Father John pointed his finger at the bearded intruder.

'Well, you're lucky, so, because my man really is dead, so there!'

'What man is dead, where? Tell me before I excommunicate you.'

Jerry sat down to gather his wits, while momentarily regretting that he had not long taken the pledge not to drink. Doorstep, his guide dog, was without doubt the best thing that could have happened to him. The dog, nice and comfortable in its new home, refused to go out after dark. Thereby depriving Jerry of the guide he wanted after a night at O'Shea's pub. And drinking alone, Jerry discovered, was no fun at all. Still, he did wonder if a small whiskey could have calmed his thoughts after what he had just found.

Father John calmed him down by reassuring him that the man in the confessional was only asleep. Even so, Jerry excitedly kept repeating himself about the dead body, until Father John got him to realise they were talking about different people.

Jerry, calmer now, tried again. 'I was checking the water level at the church's boundary when I noticed a line of old stones sticking up in the mud. In the middle was a large, flat stone with some kind of figure on it. I knelt on top of it for a closer look, thinking it was buried treasure or the like. As I did so, the stone cracked in two. Holy mother of God, Father, I wish I had been born without the curiosity. I pushed the broken stone away, hoping to find some treasure, but instead I found a body.'

Father John frowned. 'Have you started drinking, and imagining things again?'

Jerry returned a glazed thinking stare. 'I don't think so, Father. Wouldn't I know if I had?'

Father John refused to venture further into Jerry's memory. Getting concerned, he asked calmly, 'Was it a man or a woman?'

'Sure, how could I tell? It was all bone.'

'Bone? Did you say bone? Do you mean it was a skeleton?'

'Yes, a bony skeleton it is.'

'Since when in the name of all the saints is a skeleton a body?'

'Well, it used to be, so it's the same difference.'

Father John tried to think, a process not helped by the sound of a man with a wasp caught in his nose coming from the confessional. 'I'll phone the Garda to let them know what you have found. Just let me wake this fella, then we can walk over to the field and wait for them there.'

Father John squelched through the mud behind Jerry until they came face to face with what looked like an old stone coffin. The rising water from the stream had unearthed sections of the buried ruins of the first church built on that site.

Starting to get excited, Father John let his thoughts run ahead of him. Could Jerry's find be the grave of the blessed Saint Brendan who had come to Pucklorglin to banish—the legend said—troublesome leprechauns who promised the women of the village anything they desired. All that was asked in return was that they could stay safely hidden in the pockets of their aprons. Saint Brendan, so they say, dressed as a woman, agreed to hide them if they could make him walk on water. This he was granted, and one by one, he captured all the leprechauns in his apron and walked over the Irish Sea to England. Once there, they changed their names to pixies, causing mayhem for centuries, until they were finally repatriated back to Ireland.

Oblivious of the mud, Father John knelt by the stone, blessing himself. Chiselled on the stone lid was the figure of a man standing on wavy lines. In his hands he was holding what looked like small figures.

'The wavy lines represent water. He's walking on water! Holy mother of God, Jerry, it's your man, Saint Brendan, come back to us with the flooding of the stream.'

'He could never have walked on water, Father.'

'Jerry, he was a saint of Holy Mother church, and a miracle happened. You must have more faith.'

'Faith? Sure, I have plenty of that, Father.'

As Father John continued talking of a miracle, the more Jerry found it hard to contain himself any longer. Gulping for air, he all but exploded into laughter, releasing suppressed tears that streamed down his face.

'That may be, Father,' he pointed at the sacred remains, 'but how could he do it with only his feet?'

Looking closer at the muddy skeleton, Father John realised it had no leg bones. Feet, yes, but leg bones, no.

Jerry tried to control himself, saying, 'Walking on water is one thing, Father, but how his feet stay on, that's the real miracle, sure it is.'

News spread fast about the saint's remains being found. By the next morning, Saint Jude's Church was inundated with the press, fascinated by the potential discovery of the saint who once rid Ireland of leprechauns.

Photos of the skeleton appeared in the Irish Gazette, with the headline, "The Legless Saint Who Walked On Water". Those without faith, laughed. The believers, believed. And Bishop Kelly was hopping mad that the press were making his diocese a laughing stock.

To Father John's great relief, archaeologists from Dublin were invited to inspect the skeleton, and they assured him that indentations in the inner wood coffin proved that there had been leg bones present. The mystery was, where had they disappeared to?

'I know exactly where they are,' said Kathleen, with an expression that could curdle milk. 'Someone has taken them, thinking they were worth money.'

'I hope you're wrong, Kathleen. Mind you, the candle box in the church is empty again. And I filled it three times this week.' The priest sighed. 'I can't see who would want candles, or think that old bones would be worth money, for that matter. I don't like speaking ill of anybody, until the truth be known. Even so, I hope the blaggard is found soon.'

'Missing bones and candles, Father. It's a mystery, to be sure. I'll ask Mary Muldoon to keep her ear to the ground. She might pick up a bit of gossip in the shop.'

'Good idea, Kathleen. I'll be off to have a chat with the musicians in the field, to see if they have seen anything strange going on.'

Father John wandered around the mini homestead that housed the musicians who were to perform at the festival. Scanning the faces around him, he looked for the sleeping youth from the church.

'Hello, Father, what can we do for you?' an ethereal voice called to him.

Turning this way and that, Father John struggled to locate the owner of the voice.

'I'm here, Father.'

'Here? Where is here?'

'Under the tree. I'm doing my yoga. This is the Sirsha-Asana position, it increases blood flow and oxygen to the scalp.'

'You can call it what you like, I call it standing on your head. Just make sure you don't get brain damage, or is it too late already?'

'You should try it sometime, Father, and discover the good it does for yourself. Anyway, what can I do for you? Would you like a couple of free tickets for the concert?'

'Thank you, but no thank you. I'm too busy with those jackeen journalists from Dublin. Do you know what they say in today's paper? "Pucklorglin saint with no legs walked on water." It makes us look like a real bunch of eejits, so it does. Now tell me, do you know anything about those missing leg bones?'

'I can't help you there, Father. Organising the festival has taken all my time. I'll keep my eyes open for you, though.'

'That's good of you. Let me know if you see anything, will you?' *I might be lucky. The only problem is, will he really keep his eyes open?*

Father John tried talking to the other performers, but they were too busy rehearsing for the concert to discuss missing bones.

As he was leaving the field, a small boy appeared from

behind a caravan. 'Mister, will you give me a pound to tell you where the bones are?'

Sunday Mass was full to bursting, what with the extra journalists, archaeologists, visitors to the music festival, and the parishioners of Pucklorglin; all waiting in suspense to discover the mystery of the missing leg bones. Father John kept them waiting. First, he welcomed everyone and gave thanks for the safe return of Saint Brendan's legs. 'Which is a miracle in its own way.'

'Here we go again,' said Kevin Brady, the turf account. 'The best show in town is about to begin.'

'The culprit, I say the culprit, because it was just a playful exploit from someone who lives in the village.'

Everyone in the church turned and looked suspiciously at each other. The congregation were on the edge of their seats, as the press cameras flashed in anticipation of the awaited disclosure.

'She took the bones and left them under the statue of Saint Francis. We know this to be true, as we have a witness. A young lad sold—*told* me that he saw what looked like a long mop with two handles going into the church. The bone thief was Doorstep, Jerry Keogh's dog.'

'I keep telling you, Father,' piped up Jerry Keogh. 'That Doorstep is a good Catholic, so she is.'

Father John had to agree. Turning to face the altar, he had a silent word of thanks to the man upstairs. Then, to the congregation's surprise, a small group of singers from the festival, accompanied by guitars and tambourines, opened the Mass with *Here Comes the Sun.*

Everybody joined in, including Doorstep, who howled the loudest.

'What a great end to the mystery of the missing leg bones, Kathleen. This whole thing has put Pucklorglin on the map. And, what with the fee from the Irish Times, and a TV documentary on the life of Saint Brendan, we can get the roof repaired. Faith's a great thing, is it not?'

'It is, Father, and we will be needing a bit more, when it comes to growing roses.' Kathleen raised her eyebrows. 'Have you seen the flowers Jerry left in the church?'

Standing in front of the statue of Saint Francis, Father John looked fondly at Jerry's flowers. A finer bunch of dandelions he had never seen. *A weed is only a weed if you want it to be. And even a weed can lie too deep for tears.*

The following day, the travelling musicians' vans vacated the fields, moving on to places new. Father John found a lit candle in the church with a note beside it. The note thanked him and the God man for giving them light on the road ahead.

EASTER

Kathleen was spending the day with her sister, which gave Father John the peace he needed to write his Easter sermon. However, apart from some doodles, the page in front of him remained blank. Father John chewed on the end of his biro. The inspiration for his Easter sermon was proving difficult, and he blamed Mary Muldoon. And, to make matters worse, he couldn't stop sneezing.

I bet it's those flowers Jerry brought in from the garden. He removed them, but his sneezing continued. Closing his eyes for inspiration didn't help, and to top it all, his throat started to hurt.

Apart from feeling under the weather, he was still angry at what he had seen in Mary Muldoon's shop. When he first saw it, he thought he was seeing things. It wasn't until he removed his glasses that he knew he wasn't.

For there, on the box of an Easter egg, was a picture of the risen Christ. Worse was to come. Rather than the usual golden bells hanging around the chocolate bunnies' necks, there were holy medals.

Suddenly, rather than blocking his thoughts, this chocolate image started to give him the inspiration he needed for his sermon. He wrote his title. *True Perspective at Easter.*

Hmmm, I could place a strong emphasis on holy medals strung around the necks of chocolate rabbits. This will have them fidgeting in their seats by the time I'm finished.

Giving full vent to his pen, in between sneezing, he scrawled across the page. Soon, however, the sneezing got too much, and he went to make himself a hot drink.

Back in his office, trying to make himself comfortable, Father John sipped the hot lemon drink that was supposed to alleviate all cold symptoms. But it didn't seem to help. Only once he'd taken two paracetamol washed down with a small tot of brandy to help them on their way, did he start to feel a little better. But it didn't last long, so he repeated the dose. This had a more desired effect, and his creativity was now in full flow, thanks to his own remedy for the common cold.

Not long after returning to his bolt of inspiration on the evils of chocolate, Father John was interrupted by the ring of his phone.

'Good morning, Father. It's Mary from the shop. I hope I'm not disturbing you?'

Hearing Mary Muldoon's voice reminded him again of her unholy Easter display. He started to bristle at an imaginary vision of the church pews filled up with an army of melting chocolate rabbits.

'Rabbits,' he blurted out.

'Rabbits, Father?'

'Yes, I mean no, not rabbits, not chocolate rabbits.'

'Oh, we have plenty of them for Easter. Would you like me to add one to your order?'

Father John was normally a placid man, but this question touched a nerve. It was only a fit of sneezing that saved him from saying something he might regret.

'The answer is no to the chocolate, thank you Mary, or have

you forgotten it's still Lent?'

'How could I forget that, Father, what with all the holy medals in the shop at the moment?'

Father John did wonder if she was trying to annoy him, but before he could answer, she spoke again.

'I only rang to let you know that we're doing our deliveries early today as we have a promotion in the shop. We have to take part, as it's organized by the grocery chain. God knows what costume they will make us wear this time with their mad ideas. Last time we had to dress as sausages. "Farmer Richards' Sizzling Sausages." I couldn't eat a sausage for months after that. And, to cap it all, they were not even Irish sausages, but made in England.'

Not feeling up to talking about sausages, Father John was brief. 'Deliver when you like, I'm here all day.'

'Thank you, Father.'

No sooner had he replaced the receiver than the phone rang again. Then the doorbell, followed by the postman, and yet more phone calls. By the time he'd dealt with all the interruptions, his head was pounding, and he ached all over. Making himself another lemon drink laced with brandy, he increased his dose of paracetamol, and started again to write his sermon.

Easter, he began, *is all about the true spiritual and mystical significance of the risen Christ. Not grocery chains putting sacred medals on chocolate rabbits.*

His creativity was now reaching a high point, but the constant interruptions from the phone ringing were seriously impeding its flow. By the time he'd finished listening to the woes and tribulations of his parishioners, his inspirational surge had faded.

There was only one thing for it. Stuffing his pockets with pens, paper, paracetamol, and his hip flask, he decided to finish his sermon in the church.

Lighting a candle to Saint Teresa gave Father John an idea. Pouring some brandy into the little metal cup of the hip flask, he then held it over the candle's glowing flame. The warm brandy seared through him, he started to feel better again, so he had a couple more before making himself comfortable in the confessional box.

Turning on the electric heater under his chair had the desired effect. The warm air blew up his trouser legs, and the brandy warmed the rest of him. He closed his eyes and tried to think about his sermon. But the combination of heat, pills and alcohol sent him into a dream-infested sleep, where rabbits were chasing him through the village, shouting, *"Look at our medals, Father, Father, Father."*

Father John woke with a start, still hearing his name being called. Stumbling from the confessional box, he saw a giant rabbit running up the aisle of the church. Rubbing his eyes at the furry apparition, he looked again, but it had totally disappeared.

Instead, he saw Mrs O'Shea, who polishes the church brass, that found him, huddled under one of the pews sweating profusely, his face as red as a tomato.

'Is it still there?' he asked.

'Is what still there, Father?'

'The giant rabbit, getting his revenge on me.'

'There, there, Father, no one's here. Now take hold of my arm, and we'll go back to the presbytery. You don't look at all well.'

But try as she might, he refused to budge, until Kathleen returned from visiting her sister. Then, working together, they finally got him back to the presbytery. The doctor was called, who quickly diagnosed that Father John's cold had turned into flu. His delirium was the result of an accidental overdose of paracetamol and alcohol. Within an hour he was being supervised in hospital.

'What in the name of all things sensible made you take all those pills and alcohol?' Kathleen scolded. 'I was only gone for one day to see my poor sister, and I come back to find you like this.'

Father John, propped up in his hospital bed, wanted to say that he thought taking the pills and brandy was a good idea at the time, but thought better of it. 'How is your sister?'

'She's a saint, Father. How she puts up with that miserable husband of hers is a miracle, so it is. He never stops talking about his health. My sister tells people not to ask how he is, because he'll tell you. She told me that even though she had no respect for him, she doesn't have any guilt, because she always airs his washing for him.'

'Is he a sick man, then?'

'No, not at all, Father. He's a picture of health. He just wants attention, so he does.'

Father John's expression changed to a vacant stare. 'Sounds as though she will have to listen to his moaning for a time yet.'

Kathleen continued, 'I reminded her of Mammy telling us of

that poor nun and her ulcerated knees, and she soon perked up. What would we do without our martyrs?'

'Not a lot, Kathleen, which reminds me, Easter Sunday is nearly upon us, and there is a lot to organize.'

'Everything is under control at Saint Jude's, Father, there's nothing to worry about. The church is sparkling since Mrs O'Shea cleaned the brass, and her daughter has filled the whole church with flowers. All your vestments are pressed and ready, so when you come home, you can concentrate on your Easter sermon.'

Just hearing Kathleen mention the Easter sermon created the image of a giant rabbit running up the aisle of the church in Father John's mind.

'You look tired. I'll be off now, Father. All is going well, you don't have to worry about a thing, just get yourself better.'

Kathleen had no sooner gone than Mary Muldoon's son, Ronan, arrived by his bedside with a bag of grapes. 'Hello, Father. Me ma sent you some grapes, and said she hopes you're feeling better. I called on the day you were taken bad and left your order on the porch. If only I had tried the church, I might have been able to help. I'm sorry, Father, but I was in a hurry, what with the promotion people and all. And I was wearing a costume for the promotion. I looked a right eejit altogether in that thing, I can tell you.'

'You were the rabbit?'

'What rabbit is that, Father?'

'You in your costume for the shop promotion.'

'Not me. I had to dress up as a large bottle. Our promotion

was for Mr Magician the kitchen cleaner. Buy one, get one free. We sold loads.'

'If it wasn't you, who in the name of God was it?'

'Probably the Easter Bunny,' said Ronan jokingly.

A piercing '*What*?' echoed down the hospital ward.

'Did I say something to upset you, Father?'

Looking at the concerned expression on Ronan's face, Father John was sorry at losing his temper. 'Not at all, not at all. I think the medication has affected my hearing.'

'Try gargling with a drop of brandy. That should clear it.'

Father John's eyes started to glaze over as he tried to equate gargling with brandy and its benefits for the loss of hearing.

Raising his voice, making sure he could be heard, Ronan spoke slow and steady. 'I must be going now, Father. I hope your hearing improves. If you need a lift back home, just tell Kathleen and I'll pick you up.' He handed over a parcel. 'Oh, I nearly forgot. Ma said to give you this.'

After Ronan had gone, Father John sat in bed, staring into space, wondering what he had seen in the church. *If it wasn't Ronan in a rabbit costume, what in the name of God was it?*

'With all the medication you were taking, it's amazing you only saw one rabbit,' exclaimed Kathleen as she escorted a much-recovered Father John into the presbytery. 'Now that you're home, forget about rabbits. You have a busy day tomorrow.'

'You're right, of course, Kathleen. I'll just pop over to the church with a copy of my Easter sermon and run through it with the man upstairs.'

The church was peaceful and serene. Mrs O'Shea's daughter had made the flower displays a welcoming sight. Standing in front of the altar, Father John was pleased to be home.

'Well,' he began, 'I nearly ruined Easter. You arrived just in time. Mind you, a week's stay in a hospital was a hard rap on the knuckles. And if you don't mind me asking, was it yourself who sent the bloody rabbit?' Father John breathed in the sweet smell of narcissus. 'If you did, you had your reasons, I suppose.'

Turning the pages of his sermon, his pen scratched through as many lines as he added new ones. Reading aloud, the altered text spun happily from the page. 'Yes, that will do nicely. Thank you for your help, as usual.' Father John made the sign of the cross, which made him feel hungry. *Think I'll have a hot cross bun for tea. Perfect.*

Looking at the Easter queue winding round the church waiting to take Holy Communion, Father John knew, as a great many of the waiting parishioners knew, that this was their first visit since last Easter. He chuckled at the guilt on their faces. *They all look as though they fear the Garda might arrest them any minute.*

The winding queue soon returned to their pews, their spirituality renewed with promises never to let their Catholic duty slip again. Promises that would be forgotten by the following Sunday.

The congregation fell silent as Father John mounted the pulpit, ready to give his sermon. He began with the Easter story from the scriptures, saying how that was the true meaning of the season.

Feeling that Easter's religiosity was established, Father John continued, 'Chocolate rabbits. You can see them everywhere. Hopping over the pews, running up the aisle, rattling holy medals around their necks.' The congregation sat wondering what this had to do with Easter, while Kathleen looked around the church, expecting to see them.

'Easter eggs are given as a symbol of rebirth, and rabbits definitely have God's gift for that.'

Everybody laughed, as he continued, 'And Mary's shop didn't let us down. There were so many rabbits that I couldn't resist them. Thinking they needed a home,' he pointed to a large box, 'I brought them back with me. Happy Easter to you all.'

Then, blessing the congregation, Father John told the children to line up in front of the altar.

Joining the children, he gave each a gold-foil-wrapped rabbit, with a holy medal hanging around its neck.

Back at the presbytery, Father John remembered the parcel Ronan had given him at the hospital. Inside was a box with a chocolate rabbit inside, bedecked with not one, but two holy medals. A note from Mary said that Ronan had found the other one by the church on the day he was taken ill.

God moves in mysterious ways, that's for sure. That giant rabbit I saw in the church, I know was only a hallucination. The spare medal? I wonder where that came from? Father John opened the box and removed the gold foil, exposing the glistening chocolate beneath. There was only one course of action to be taken in a tempting situation like this. So, with that conviction in mind, he removed the remaining foil from the rabbit, bit off its chocolate ears and ate them.

IT'S THE LITTLE THINGS

The discovery of the blessed Saint Brendan's remains in Saint Jude's grounds had reached the ears of his Holy Father the Pope in Rome. As well as Father John's knowledge in deciphering the figure on the coffin's lid, his handling of the whole affair was admired and approved of by the Vatican.

'Kathleen, you'll never guess.'

'Correct, Father. So tell me.'

'I've been invited to a cultural gathering at the Vatican. Holy mother of God.' He paused. 'I'll be in the presence of the Holy Father himself! Put the kettle on, will you, Kathleen, and make my tea hot and sweet.'

For a moment, Kathleen couldn't speak. '*You* are going to Rome? Who would have thought it? I'll take your best suit to the cleaners and get you some new shoelaces. You must look your best meeting the Holy Father himself in the flesh.'

'New shoelaces? The ones I have work perfectly well. Anyway, who in God's name will be looking at my shoelaces?'

Kathleen stared at Father John as though he was one of Saint Jude's hopeless cases. 'It's the little things that matter, Father. There's always someone who will notice the little things.'

When Bishop Kelly was told the news, he said the diocese would pay all the expenses incurred on his trip to Rome, and would arrange for a deputy until he returned.

The bishop had told Father John that he had the very person in mind.

'He's not long ordained, and is, so I have been told, a whizz-kid with technology. I'll ask him to do a talk on using computers while he is in Pucklorglin. It might encourage more parishioners to use them. Then we can send the parish magazine and monthly newsletter online and save on the printing and postage.'

Well, good luck to you with that one. Father John's reply had been short. 'That's an interesting idea, your Grace.'

'All *you* have to do when you are with His Eminence,' Bishop Kelly said, 'is make sure the parish of Pucklorglin and the diocese leave their intellectual mark. We don't want those foreign fellas thinking we're a bunch of eejits now, do we?'

Two weeks later, Father John's suit was returned from the dry cleaners, and Kathleen had purchased a pair of new black shoelaces, along with a tin of shoe polish, and a new duster to go with them.

His suitcase all packed, Father John double checked he had included everything on his list. A quick clean and polish of his shoes, and he was ready to go. Waiting for the taxi to arrive to take him to the airport, Kathleen fussed around him as if he was going to the moon.

'Are you sure you have everything, Father? Passport, your ticket, money, sunglasses?'

'Sunglasses? What would I be doing with sunglasses? I'm going to Rome, not the strand.'

'Exactly! You said it. Going to Rome. Those Italians always wear sunglasses. Sure, they do.' Sniffing the air, Kathleen changed the subject. 'I put some cheese sandwiches in your holdall. They will keep until tonight, just in case you're hungry. You never know what you'll be getting to eat in those foreign places.'

'Thank you, Kathleen.' *I don't think I'll be needing them.* 'That was a kind thought.'

'Ah, it's just a little thing. You never know if you will be needing them.'

'Now, I'm only gone for a week. There's nothing to worry about, and my deputy will be here tomorrow. As you know, he was only ordained a few months ago, so a week in Pucklorglin will teach him a thing or two.' Father John chuckled to himself. *And good luck to you, lad, if you're going to try and get the Catholic Women's League to attend a computer talk.* 'You know, Kathleen, Bishop Kelly has his mind set on saving money by using a computer.'

'Saving money? The bishop? Me mammy would say short arms and long pockets to that. But don't worry yourself. I'll help your deputy all I can.' Turning him round in a circle, she did a final inspection. 'Your hair looks better after you getting it cut. You just enjoy yourself, Father, and one little thing. Please give the Holy Father my regards.'

'Your regards?'

The look of determination on Kathleen's face spoke volumes. 'Yes, I can't see why you can't give His Holiness my best wishes.'

To Father John's relief, the taxi arrived before a discussion on the Pope's time for small talk made him miss his flight.

Relaxing in the back of the taxi, Father John felt in a holiday mood. All the little worries he had about going away started to disappear. *Everything in my diary has been seen to. All those little annoying jobs finished. Nothing for Kathleen to worry about. She's right, it's the little things that count.*

Everything in the presbytery was cleaned, polished, and organised for the arrival of Father John's deputy. Kathleen wondered what he would be like. Not many young men were joining the priesthood nowadays, what with satellite dishes and trips to the moon. Now they questioned where God really was. Father John said that he was in everything. But most of all in our hearts.

A loud knocking on the presbytery door made Kathleen jump. Opening it, she thought it was one of those fellows who deliver express letters, as a man stood by his motorbike, clad in a black leather suit and matching black helmet.

Removing his helmet, her visitor smiled. 'Hello, I'm Father Matthew, Father John's deputy while he is in Rome.'

Taking one look at his dusty appearance, Kathleen said, 'You can take your boots off before you come in. I've just polished the floors.'

'Oh, you didn't have to bother on my account. Sure, I was born on a farm.'

'That's as may be, Father, but the presbytery is not a barn.'

Although Kathleen meant her remark to be light-hearted,

Father Matthew did not take it as such. He wasn't what Kathleen was expecting.

'Would you like a cup of tea and a piece of cake after your journey? I made it especially for you.' Kathleen proudly tried to usher Father Matthew into the newly-polished parlour.

'Not for me, thank you. I never eat cake. Could you show me to the office? I have to send an email.'

'Emails, is it? What's wrong with the post?'

'I never use the post. It's much too slow.' His 'too slow' was puffed out with a *what are we waiting for* look on his face.

Deciding to put his abruptness down to first day nerves, Kathleen said, 'Follow me. I think Father John keeps the computer in a cupboard in the office. He never uses it. He enjoys talking to the parishioners in the village when he posts his letters.'

'Letters are a thing of the past. This is the big technical age.' His tone suggested that he had invented technology himself, singlehanded.

Kathleen kept her lips firmly closed as she watched Father Matthew sorting out plugs and sockets to get the computer working.

'I'll have this up and running in no time. Which reminds me, has a small parcel arrived for me from Bishop Kelly? It will be the leaflets for a talk I'm giving on using the computer for beginners.'

'Not so far, Father. Would you like me to type your letters while you sort that lot out?'

Kathleen's offer went unanswered. The awkward silence was only broken by the phone ringing.

'Saint Jude's Church, how can I help you?' Kathleen was silent for a moment. 'Holy mother of God, are you sure? No, it's too late—he's already left for Rome.'

Trying to concentrate on anything after the phone call was impossible. Although the dry cleaners apologised for the mix up, there was nothing she could do. *Sacred heart of Jaysus, who would have thought the cleaners still had hold of one of Father Frank's suits, and worse, to deliver it by mistake, thinking it was Father John's! I bet Father John packed the suit without checking it, and he's so much taller than Father Frank was.*

She thought about the nun scrubbing the floors with the ulcerated knees, as she contemplated walking to Rome with his suit. The only consolation she had was that now that his trousers would be shorter, his shoes would be more visible. *At least they have new laces.*

Father John was shown to his room by a jolly Irish nun from County Clare.

'I'm Sister Dymphna. If there's anything you want during your stay, just ask. Did you have a good flight, Father?'

'I did, apart from the turbulence. Which in itself didn't bother me, but your man next to me couldn't keep still, and on account of his fidgeting, his cup of coffee landed in my lap. I need to change my suit, as this one's still damp.'

'Bad luck, Father. I'll leave you to it then.' Sister Dymphna looked at her watch. 'If you're quick, the dry cleaners could collect it. I will make it express so it will be ready in the morning for you. Just leave it outside of the door.'

'That's good of you, Sister, thanks.'

Leaving the suit as he was asked, he started unpacking his case, and changed into his other suit. It didn't feel right.

Father John stood in front of the mirror, eyeing the half-mast trousers and the short arms of the jacket. Momentarily shocked, it took a few minutes for the penny to drop. *It's not my suit.*

This revelation, and what to do about it, left him momentarily without a solution. Remembering his other suit, Father John quickly opened the door of his room, but it had already been collected for dry cleaning. To make matters worse, the first item on his itinerary was a welcome gathering, and group audience with the Holy Father. There were no options left. He knelt down for a chat with the man upstairs.

Well now, this is a right mess I'm after getting myself into. Sacred heart of Jesus, what can I do looking like this? I'm about to meet your representative on Earth. Wearing this suit. Have you any suggestions, Lord?'

Although Father Matthew had only been at the presbytery for a few days, Kathleen was beginning to think that the rest of the week with him couldn't come quick enough. Before early morning Mass he jogged the length of Ireland. Then, having only a banana, followed by green tea in the morning, took away all pleasure of cooking a healthy breakfast for him. Not to mention the hours he spent on the computer, leaving her extra duties with the parishioners.

Father Matthew didn't look up as Kathleen put his morning coffee on the desk. As usual, he was tip tapping away on the computer keys.

'Are you looking for God on that thing, or what?'

He didn't answer, so Kathleen wondered if perhaps he was.

Without taking his eyes off the screen, he finally replied, 'You should learn how to use one, Kathleen. It will help you get things done, like online shopping. I will cover these points in my talk.'

'How in God's name can I choose your bananas online? Not to mention meeting people in Mary Muldoon's shop. The old people in the village love to have a friendly word. It stops them feeling lonely and cut off.'

'That's a sad fact of life, Kathleen, but it's the way forward for us all. Little things like choosing your own bananas won't exist soon. You'll have to jump into the modern world or else you will be left behind. I hope you're coming to my talk, by the way.'

'I will, *if* I have the time.'

'You're a terrible procrastinator, Kathleen, always putting things off.'

Kathleen was silent. *I never put things off in my life! There aren't enough hours in the day working here as it is! The house doesn't clean itself, and the fairies don't cook the meals. And all Father Matthew can do is look at the computer screen. God help the sick and dying if he arrives on his motorbike, with the communion cup bouncing around in the panniers on the back.*

The phone rang at the same time as the doorbell. Kathleen chose the phone, hoping it was Father John ringing from Rome. She was disappointed, however. The voice on the other end was the bishop's secretary, who, once they started to talk, never stopped. By the time Kathleen got off the phone, she had forgotten all about the doorbell having rung.

With the suit jacket open, and the cuffs of his shirt pulled down so as not to show his wrists, Father John prayed that his socks would stay up, giving the illusion that his trousers appeared longer than they were. Looking in the mirror at the final effect, the only thing that came to mind was Farmer Logan's scarecrow.

In God's great scheme of things, the length of my trousers doesn't have a place. Things are what they are, so I'll get on with it.

With this thought in mind, he proudly set off for the reception, and to meet the Holy Father himself.

The audience chamber had a superficial air of grandeur about it. *All that glitters is not gold.* Father John looked around him, aware that his suit had been noticed. Nor was he blind to the expensive tailored suits that some of the other Fathers were wearing.

Everybody waited in anticipation for the Pope to arrive. When his private door opened, a small man dressed in simple white robes entered. His presence filled the room. Father John stood in line, waiting to be introduced. When his turn came, a feeling of peace drifted over him. Their conversation was brief in comparison to the others. And he did notice the Holy Father look down at his feet.

He must have noticed my trousers. I only hope I haven't let Pucklorglin down.

As the reception ended, Father John was approached by one of the papal staff. 'The Holy Father asks that you remain. He has some questions to ask you.'

By the time the bishop's secretary had finally got off the phone, Kathleen started on her list of things to do. The Catholic Women's League summer outing, ringing the florist to order flowers for Sunday Mass, wanting the church to look its best to welcome Father John home. Then the Fly with the Bees children's group, hosted by Jerry Keogh. *That's a good start, three things off the list. What's next?*

Deep in thought, Kathleen jumped as Father Matthew burst into the kitchen, red faced and holding a soggy parcel.

'The bishop's leaflets for the computer talk, Kathleen—they were left on the doorstep in the pouring rain. They're soaked! The delivery note says no one at home. If you had said you were out, I would have waited for them.'

Kathleen thought it better not to say that she was busy with other things at the time. Calmly, she said, 'Don't worry about the leaflets, they'll be fine. I'll dry them out for you. It's a pity you can't send emails telling them what day you're giving your talk, what with none of them having computers. Leave it with me, Father, Peter McAlarney will deliver them for you.'

Father Matthew's red face had cooled down to a pale pink. 'Who is Peter McAlarney?'

'The postman. He'll pop a flyer in the letterboxes with the post. He won't mind, it's only a little thing to ask.'

The rest of Father John's time in Rome had been enjoyable and meaningful. The exchange of cultural differences between the invited priests was very informative. Father John had felt more comfortable when his own suit was returned. There was great craic when he had told the other delegates about the unfortunate mix up. He also had the ear of the other priests with his tales of Pucklorglin. Several, especially those from largely impoverished cities, told him he was living in a fairytale place. Silently, Father John had to agree with them. Not wanting to leave out Bishop Akuma's visit, he spoke proudly about his gift to the church. This mention of a neon sign was received without comment.

Looking back as he made his way home, the highlight of his trip to Rome was the extraordinary private conversation he had with the Holy Father. As requested, he had stayed behind after the reception. *Why me? It must be the suit. He did give me a strange look. Maybe he thought it was an insult to appear dressed like that. I'll apologise first, then explain.*

By the time everyone had left, Father John's concern over the suit had run away with him. That was until the Holy Father greeted him again.

'Father John Phelan from Ireland, welcome. I wanted to talk to you.'

Here it comes, my suit.

'About the missing leg bones mystery in your parish of Pucklorglin.'

Father John, only thinking about his suit, had carried on by saying, 'I must explain, your Holiness. The coffee of the man sitting next to me,' he paused, feigning a cough, as events caught up with him, '…the leg bones? Yes, that was a strange one. Indeed it was. As you say, a mystery.'

A little confused, the Pope's face had broken into a broad smile. 'I haven't laughed so much for a long time. God forgive me, but walking across the Irish Sea with pockets full of leprechauns, honestly! Only one person I know of walked on water, and you have to have a bucket full of faith to accept how he did that. Still, miracles are good.' Father John remembered the Holy Father's eyes had momentarily closed.

'They happen all the time in Pucklorglin, your Holiness—figuratively speaking, that is. Take Doorstep, who found the missing leg bones, and Saint Patrick's blue cloak. Not to mention Wyatt Earp.'

The more Father John had reeled off the daily happenings in Pucklorglin, sprinkled with good Irish humour, the more the Holy Father had wanted to hear. And the more he heard, the more he had laughed.

'Now, I must ask you a few serious questions, Father. First, what is your opinion of Noah and the flood in Genesis?'

Perplexed, 'The children enjoy it. But we're not the only one with that tale. All the great books have a flood story.'

'And,' the Holy Father had continued, 'what about the parable of the loaves and fishes?'

'Well now, this is where faith comes in, to be sure. But you would be needing a shedload on that one. When I was a boy, me mammy always said Jaysus took a risk with that many people. And that she would have died with shame if the food had run out, and there wasn't enough to go round.'

The Pope had smiled. 'Are you always so direct, Father?'

'Me mammy also said, tell the truth and shame the devil.'

'You had a wise mother. I ask these questions because we are now in a new age, with space travel and science running ahead of our thoughts.'

Father John had watched a shadow of uncertainty drift over the Holy Father's face.

'Well,' he had answered, 'if by space travel, we do meet little green men, we'll welcome them. Sure, they will all be God's creatures.'

'Let's hope you're right, Father. Now, my last question to you is, how will you keep the faith in people's hearts?'

'Sure, that's easy to answer. Stand back and listen to them. Don't ram a bowl of cabbage down a child's throat. He'll hate it for the rest of his life. And believe in yourself.'

Father John had ended his personal audience with the Pope by explaining about his suit. It took him some time, though, as the Holy Father at first thought it was going to be another Irish tale.

The last few days of his time in Rome, Father John popped in and out of unassuming church doors, that once opened displayed architectural splendour inside, with great art staring out from their walls. Surrounded with all this grandeur, he lit a candle and allowed his inward eye to rest happily upon Saint Jude's.

All the sightseeing of ruins, great pillars and porticos, forums, and statues of ancient Romans who thought things would never change made him realise his own journey. Now it was time to return to Saint Jude's, and he couldn't wait.

After an incident-free flight back, Father John relaxed in the presbytery's cosy kitchen.

'Then the Holy Father asked questions about Saint Brendan walking leprechauns over the Irish Sea. "Holy mother of God," he said, "no wonder his leg bones were missing after all that walking." The Pope has a great sense of humour, that's for sure.'

Father John, knowing of Kathleen's loyalty to Saint Brendan, thought it best to give a shortened version of that part of his conversation with the Holy Father.

Kathleen, however, had conflicted feelings on how to take these remarks about Pucklorglin's only saint, so changed the subject.

'Did he notice your suit?'

'He did, so, but I explained about the mix up.'

'Such a little thing like that could have ruined things. It was the same with the bananas.'

Suits to bananas? 'Kathleen, you're talking in tongues. Bananas?'

'Father Matthew said I should learn how to use the computer to do my shopping online, like buying bananas.'

'Pay no heed to him. He's new at the job. As for buying bananas online, we only have Mary's shop, and I can't see her getting a computer. What would we all do without a little gossip? Did many show up for his talk?'

'About half a dozen, including Flynn and Hannah, who kept interrupting, asking when the tea and cake would be served. In the end I felt sorry for him.'

'You did what you could, Kathleen. Tomorrow we will be back to normal.'

Kathleen smiled. Things had started to settle already. 'I always believed in the little things making a difference, Father. Perhaps I was wrong. I'm thinking it would be better to concentrate on the big things instead.'

'No, Kathleen. Stick to your way of doing things. A little word, a little smile, a little gesture, makes all the difference in the world. Which reminds me, there's one other thing the Holy Father asked me. He said, how nice to see new shoelaces these days, and asked if I'd bought them especially for the visit?'

'He noticed the shoelaces?'

'He did. So just you carry on the way you are, Kathleen. The little things are the building blocks to kinder things.'

Father John did enjoy his visit to Rome, but nothing compared to sitting in his church discussing things with the man upstairs. *I think perhaps you can forgive me. Even if the Holy Father didn't actually say that about my shoelaces, I'm sure he must have been thinking it, the amount of time he spent studying my shoes.*

GABRIEL

Kathleen checked the names on her list. 'Well, the minibus will be full. We have a good crowd wanting to come on the summer outing to Rosebeigh this Sunday, Father. It's always very popular. Sure, Father Frank loved his day by the sea, so he did, poor man.'

'His death was a real tragedy,' Father John sighed. 'Who would have thought such a thing could happen in Pucklorglin.' *There again, where else?* 'One thing's for certain, Kathleen, you never know what's round the corner. He will be well remembered. We'll all say a prayer for him at Mass on Sunday before we set off. Which reminds me, I had better ring the garage and book a service for the church car. We're bound to have a few more on the day wanting to come.'

'You carry on, so, Father. I have plenty to do in the kitchen.'

After making an appointment with the garage, Father John, on looking out of his office window, felt an ominous fear of the inevitable when he saw Bridget Mooney's son, Ginger, heading towards the church.

Rushing to get to the church before Ginger Mooney did, so he could lock everything of value out of temptation's way, was a well-practised drill. Every door, drawer and cupboard in sight had to be secured. Ginger was as light fingered as his father, but quicker.

The problem was, Father John couldn't find the church keys.

'Kathleen,' he yelled, 'have you seen the church keys? Especially the one for the collection box.'

Kathleen raised her eyes to heaven. *God forgive me for even thinking of swearing, but how many times this week has he lost his frigging keys?*

'Perhaps the little people have taken them, Father, or they're where you left them before.'

'Where I left them before what?'

'Before you lost them. Or you could tie a piece of string around a chair leg, and say a prayer to Saint Anthony. He'll find them for you. It always works for me.'

'Kathleen, you're talking in riddles. I have to find them quickly. The Mooneys are back, and their son Ginger will be in the church anytime now. I need to lock up the candle box.'

'What in the name of Saint Patrick would he be wanting with candles?'

'They're portable, what else?'

Kathleen nodded. 'You go and look in your office and check your pockets. I'll search in here. Found them, Father, they were under the parish magazine. It's as I said, the little folk must have put them there.'

Father John mumbled something under his breath that he'd never say in the pulpit on a Sunday. Then, with the retrieved keys, he ran over to the church, locking up anything that could fit into a pocket. He was just about finished when Ginger Mooney walked through the heavy church door, dragging one of his sisters by the hand.

'Well, well now, Ginger Mooney, what can I be doing for

you today?'

'Two things, Father,' sniffed Ginger, wiping his nose on his shirt sleeve. 'Ma sent me to tell you our da died while we were away, and will you come to see her?'

On hearing about the death of Ginger's father, memories of the dead man crowded before Father John's eyes. 'I'm sorry to hear that, Ginger. Tell your mammy that I will say a Mass for him. He won't be forgotten.' Not that Father John could ever forget his face, alive or dead, for every time he said Mass, the stone carving of a gargoyle that stared down on him from the altar column was the spitting image of Mickey Mooney himself. 'What did he die of?'

'Of a Tuesday, Father. We were at the races when he started to feel bad. Ma was telling fortunes to the rich ones from Dublin, and Da was helping himself.'

'Helping himself to what?'

'I meant helping me mammy.'

'I'll try and believe you. Thousands wouldn't. How long is it since your last confession?'

Ginger said he couldn't remember, but that his mammy would know. 'You can ask her when you come over. And Mammy asked could my sister Thelma here go on the outing to Rosebeigh, after Mass on Sunday.' With this, he turned and ran, dragging his sister behind him.

The Mooneys earned their living by attending every horse fair, oyster fair, and any other fair where money was to be made. Mickey sold wooden animals that he carved. Father John was impressed by the intricate detail he put into them.

Father John had on many occasions enjoyed talking with Mickey. He was in his own way a lovable rogue, who always attended Mass when he was in the village.

Standing in front of the altar and lighting a candle in his memory, he wondered what Ginger Mooney meant by saying his father died of a Tuesday. Father John glanced up at the stone carving. 'This candle is for you, Mickey, and if you do make it to the pearly gates, I'm telling you now, don't do it. They won't fit into your caravan. Amen.'

After telling Kathleen that he was driving over to see Mrs Mooney, he then told her he'd changed his mind, and would walk instead—he did not tell her it was because he couldn't find his car keys, and he had had enough of Kathleen's jibes on the subject.

Sitting comfortably in Madge Mooney's spacious caravan, Father John looked at the copious knickknacks that jostled for space on the mirrored shelves. Holy statues of the Virgin Mary, and nearly every saint in heaven stood shoulder to shoulder with trinkets of an undisclosed origin.

Madge Mooney sat surrounded by children of all ages, a large box on her lap. She handed it to Father John. 'Mickey said to give this to you, Father.'

Suspicious of its contents, Father John asked, 'What's this then?'

'Open it and see, Father,' she said proudly.

To Father John's astonishment, in the box were two large brass candlesticks. 'These belonged to the church. Or, should I say, *belong* to the church. I saw a photo of them published in a back edition of the parish magazine just after they went missing.'

'The very same, Father,' said Madge, trying to move on quickly from his prior knowledge of the candlesticks. 'Mickey lit them every Christmas and toasted Father Frank, God rest his soul. He wanted you to have them, if anything happened to himself, so he did.'

'But they already belong to us. Or should I say Saint Jude's.'

'Ah, you're right, Father, but his dying wish was for you to enjoy them again.'

What could he say? Mickey Mooney's magnanimous gesture had the family crying at their da's generosity; with the old rogue, no doubt, looking down on them, enjoying the craic.

Madge stretched out her arms, hoping to encompass her numerous children. Tears streaked down their grubby faces. 'One more thing, Father. Just before the angels took him, he had a message for you from the other side. He said, don't worry about your loss, for Gabriel will take care of you.'

The priest was perplexed by Mickey's mystical prediction. 'Gabriel? The archangel Gabriel?'

'Who else is there? We all have a guardian angel. Yours must be Gabriel himself.'

*

Walking back to the church, Father John thought of Mickey's message to him from the other side. *What was the old eejit talking about, the other side? Other side of the bottle, more likely.* At least he could tell the bishop that the candlesticks had been returned.

The day of the outing arrived. During Mass, all you could hear was wriggling children, and the clanking of buckets and spades. Father John was in an exceptionally good mood. His sermon telling the story of Jesus walking on water carried a warning. He'd told them it was your man's trick and not to try it if anyone took the boat trip around the bay. Laughter filled the church, making Father John happy.

The minibus was full to bursting with all the extra paraphernalia for a day by the sea. Including picnic baskets, and pre-inflated rubber rings. The overflow of children all piled into the church's large old car.

'Keys, Kathleen. Where are the keys?'

'In your hand, Father.'

'Correct. Just testing you. Right, is everybody ready? Then let's be having you. Rosebeigh here we come.'

The children played on the beach, swam in the sea, and seemed not to notice that they were getting sand into their sandwiches. After ice cream and donkey rides on the strand, Kathleen noticed a sign advertising a sandcastle competition that very day, so they all set to work, building their sandcastles. Father John, seeing that everybody was having a good time, rolled up his trouser legs and paddled in the sea.

As he stared out at the vast expanse of ocean before him, Father John found Mickey Mooney coming to his mind. *The cheek of the man, lighting the candlesticks he took from the church. Then toasting Father Frank at Christmas. Still, you can't help but laugh. At least he didn't sell them. Then that message from him—what was that all about? In no way was he gifted with the third sense. Mind you, he was the seventh son of a seventh son. Or so he said. Only time itself will sort that one out.*

Shouts of 'Father, Father, come and help me with my sandcastle' jogged him back from his thoughts.

Ginger Mooney's sister, Thelma, filled and patted the sand down in her bucket, helped by Father John, who then placed the waiting turrets on the sandy mound.

'That's grand, Thelma. Now hold on a while, I've got a small Irish flag in the car.'

Thelma stuck the flag in the centre turret. It won second prize, and a chocolate ice lolly for Thelma.

What a grand day everyone had, full of fun and sea air. Kathleen helped with packing up everything from shells to buckets of salty seaweed for the journey home. Checking the sandy toed children in the back of the car, Kathleen made herself comfortable in the front seat. Father John was nearly finished checking the passenger list in the minibus before it set off for Pucklorglin.

Returning to the car, Father John did a quick head count,

before turning to Kathleen. 'Right, all present and correct. Are we all set to go? Keys, please.'

Kathleen rolled her eyes. 'I haven't got them, Father. You have.'

The priest grinned. 'No more jokes now. Let's have the keys.'

Silence filled the car as Father John looked at his right-hand woman, but Kathleen simply shook her head.

'Holy mother of God. You're not joking. Where are the keys?'

Kathleen gave him a rasping stare. 'Let's thank Saint Peter you don't have the keys to heaven, for none of us would get in.'

Returning to where they had been sitting, Father John sank down beside the sandcastle to think. *I know I had them, because I locked the car door after I got the flag.* But try as he might, his inward eye couldn't locate them. *Time for a chat with the man upstairs.*

Evening was creeping in, and the strand was nearly empty; the ice-cream kiosk was shutting for the day. In the distance, the donkeys were all tethered together, heading towards Father John. As they reached him, one stopped, nearly stepping on Thelma's sandcastle, before deciding to empty its bladder.

Father John narrowly escaped the torrent that shot down on the castle's flagged turrets. Watching the crumbling battlements disappearing in the donkey's never-ending flow, it didn't take long for the sandy fortress to disappear. Only the little Irish flag had remained upright, as something was in its way.

Holy mother of God. The car keys. Father John jumped up from his knees to pat the obliging animal, before sinking down again when he saw the donkey's name on the headband. Gabriel.

Back at the church, Father John knelt down for a chat with the man upstairs. 'No matter what goes wrong, things always turn out all right in the end. Thanks for a grand day. That donkey could have stopped anywhere; it was a big beach, after all.

'And, as for Mickey Mooney, I thank him for Gabriel. And to have the candlesticks back in Saint Jude's again. Amen.'

That evening, looking at the candlesticks on his desk, Father John lit the remaining stubby wax ends before pouring himself a glass of brandy. 'Well Mickey Mooney, I lost the keys and Gabriel found them. You saved the day and left me wondering how you knew. Thank you for thinking of me.'

Raising the brandy glass in the air, he added, 'Sláinte, Mickey Mooney, and thank you for your message. Rest in peace, and remember what I said, keep your hands off the pearly gates.'

FATHER FORGIVE ME

'Good morning, Father. This was on the mat,' said Kathleen, handing him a letter.

'Thank you. Oh, I see it's been delivered by hand. Did you see who dropped it by?'

'Sorry, Father, I was cutting up the pumpkin to make soup. I have a busy day today getting the hall ready for the Cubs and Brownies. They're having a Halloween-themed tea after school today.'

'That's nice.' He slid the letter from its envelope. 'Tell me, Kathleen, who is Bridget Mulligan?'

'Bridget Mulligan? What made you ask that?'

'This letter, it's from herself. She asks me to pop round this evening.'

'Well, she has just moved into the village. Her mother passed away before you arrived. All I can say is let's hope she's not like her mother.'

'What was wrong with her mother?'

'It's not for me to spread nasturtiums.'

'You mean aspersions, Kathleen.'

'As I said, Father. It's not for me.'

'Well, I'll find out for myself. I'll pop over later and see what she wants. Where does she live?'

'The cottage on the edge of Witch Hazel Wood. If I can offer some advice; don't go to her cottage, see her here at the presbytery.'

'Don't go? Why not?'

'For one, it's Halloween night, and for two, it's dark and, as I said, it's Halloween.'

Father John was silent as he tried to work out Kathleen's reasoning.

'She's a strange one. Odd things have gone on in that cottage.'

'Ah, gossip, is it? Well, I don't listen to gossip, as you well know. So, I shall be going to see Bridget Mulligan later.'

'That's up to you, then. But take your rosary with you.'

Father John made his way over to the church to prepare for confessions. *Thank God we don't have witch trials anymore. Gossip is a dangerous thing.* Making himself comfortable in the confessional box, waiting for the first sinner to arrive, he thought about Bridget Mulligan, and what she wanted to see him about. He hoped once he'd met her, he could stop whatever gossip it was that had spread through the village.

His thoughts were disturbed by the sound of footsteps heading in his direction. The first sinner in Pucklorglin had arrived.

Seamus Murphy drank too much, and he knew it. Living just around the corner from William O'Shea's pub, his favoured drinking venue, was only a short walk away. On the nights Seamus was in the pub, the barman called last orders early, hoping to cut down Seamus's alcohol consumption, and, if needed, trying to get someone to walk him home.

Seamus was eighteen when his mother told him that the Virgin Mary would always look after him if he took the pledge not to drink. 'It's the devil's brew, son,' she would say. 'And the devil claims his own in the end.'

To please his mother, and keen not to be claimed by the devil, alcohol never touched his lips during the formative years of adulthood. But as Seamus's life moved on, with his constant prayers remaining unanswered, and all his fine plans helter-skeltering downwards, he'd begun to question if his mother knew what she was talking about.

After a village trip to Lourdes, his mother had become ill and passed away. The doctor told Seamus it was a rare strain of bird flu. To which he replied that they went to Lourdes, not a bird sanctuary. Although he did remember a seagull shat on her coat. *Holy mother of God, she was killed by a seagull.*

For Seamus, this was the last straw. He removed his pledge badge, and took himself off to the pub for his first drink. But not his last.

'Father, forgive me,' Seamus began as usual, as he stared at the shadowy figure behind the grille in the confessional box. 'It's been a week since my last confession. Jaysus, it's bloody dark in here. Is that you, Father, or a cardboard cutout?'

'To answer your first request, Seamus, God always forgives the repentant sinner. Which you are not. I can smell the drink on you from here. And, as for the dark, light is not needed for the confession of your sins.'

Father John raised his eyes to heaven. Seamus was not a sinful man, just a man on a mission which he kept failing to accomplish. 'This drinking of yours has gone on for far too long. Why you bother to confess at all is a mystery. You'll be straight to the pub when you leave here.'

'Never a truer word spoken, Father. My addiction to alcohol is the cause of my drinking. You won't believe me, Father, but I don't really care for the stuff. It's become a habit since I was told of the bird flu that took me ma.'

'A habit, you call it. Is that what you want to believe, Seamus? Now, listen to me. The drink will be the ruin of you, man. Mark my words. The devil will seek you out when you least expect it, I'm telling you.'

Seamus shuddered; he could feel the eternal fire licking at his feet. 'It's hard to believe, Father, but the devil is so powerful, isn't it him that makes me drink in the first place, even when I don't want to?'

'You're right, it is hard to believe. As are all the excuses coming from you, a man who took the pledge. You must face him, Seamus, and refuse the road the devil wants you to tread, before he arrives to carry you away forever. Instead of going to O'Shea's tonight, try to stay at home. Then gradually phase out going at all. Have a hot drink and a couple of paracetamol before you go to bed. It will help you to sleep.'

'Paracetamol, you say? Never. I'm allergic to medicine ever since I was a child, so I am.'

'Then it's up to you. Go away and think of what I said. Your penance is ten decades of the rosary every evening until I see a change in you. In the name of the Father, and of the Son, and of the Holy Ghost, Amen.'

As he left the confessional, all Seamus could think about was a visitation from Hell. This thought propelled him to the pub for a drink to steady his nerves. The more he thought of Hell's heat, the more he needed to quench it.

During the evening, the landlord refused to serve him anymore. 'You had better take hold of the devil's tail, Seamus. He's the only one that could lead you home now.'

Kathleen raised her eyes to heaven. 'So you're still going to visit that Bridget Mulligan after all I said, tonight of all nights?'

'The only difference to me is that today is Tuesday, and tomorrow is Wednesday. Halloween doesn't come into it.'

Kathleen lowered her voice, looking from side to side for an unseen presence. 'I have warned you, Father. If she is anything like her mother, don't stay too long, and don't forget your rosary.'

'And have you also seen her on her broomstick flying around the village, by any chance?' Father John joked.

'I've never seen her at all, as it so happens. But I was warned about her by a very good source.'

'Would that be the gossiping source, by any chance?'

'You'll soon find out for yourself, Father. She's a strange one, and don't say you were not warned. I made you a pumpkin soup for your tea. I hope you enjoy it.' Kathleen spoke slowly, as though fully expecting it would be his last meal.

Kathleen's parting remarks did not put him off his soup. He always looked forward to trying something new. But after he had finished eating, he felt as though he had eaten a field of pumpkins, which gave him indigestion. *What in the name of heaven did Kathleen mean by saying visiting that strange one tonight of all nights? And to take my rosary?*

Bridget Mulligan lived in an old cottage on the edge of the village. Nothing inside had been changed since her grandparents departed this world over thirty years ago, leaving the cottage to their only daughter, Bridget's mother. Mrs Mulligan Senior had passed away just before Father John arrived in Pucklorglin. Her daughter had not long moved into the vacant cottage, and the village chit chat was that she took after her mother.

The Halloween festivities in the village were well under way as Father John set off. Children dressed as witches and ghouls zigzagged excitedly up and down the streets.

A cat, frightened out of its wits by all the noise, ran in front of an inebriated Seamus as he swayed back home from O'Shea's pub. Trying to avoid the cat, he tripped over his own feet, landing face down, shouting that the devil was behind him.

Hearing Seamus saying this sent the children yelling and

shrieking in every direction. In the rush not to be the devil's victim, they dropped what they were carrying, leaving the road littered with hats, broomsticks, and all the paraphernalia of the imagined living dead.

Not far from Bridget Mulligan's cottage, Father John got caught up with the excited children still shouting that the devil was behind them. Trying to calm them down didn't work. The fun was in being scared.

Going in the opposite direction to the one that the children had come from, Father John heard a soft groaning sound ahead of him. His first thought was that one of the children had got left behind. Then, in the darkness, he saw the outline of a body propped up against a wall, but he couldn't see who it was. Taking a few steps closer, he realised that one of the fleeing children had dropped a pumpkin lantern in the rush to avoid the devil. The candle inside was still alight. Father John picked it up, bringing it closer to the sleeping shape.

'Is that you, Seamus?' he asked, giving the body a good shake.

Seamus opened his eyes, only to see a bright orange face with fire burning in the sockets where the eyes should be. As Father John brought the pumpkin lantern closer, Seamus, even more fearful, tried to scream as he looked at the large cut out mouth, and fearful teeth in front of him.

'Seamus, get up, and come with me,' said Father John softly. 'You're drunk again. You had better come with me.'

Seamus, rigid with fright, couldn't move. *Father John was right! The devil has come to claim me as one of his own.*

The fear of this pending one-way journey, coupled with the drink, and the burning eyes of Hell probing deep into his alcoholic soul, made Seamus pass out.

Despite his best efforts, Father John couldn't get him on his feet. As luck would have it, a neighbour was passing, and offered to stay with Seamus until he was conscious enough to be walked home.

'That's very good of you. I'm just on my way to Bridget Mulligan's cottage. She's expecting me.'

'Bridget Mulligan's cottage, you say, Father?' the neighbour questioned him back.

'The same. I've never met her. I believe she's a recluse?'

'A recluse, is she now? I don't know about that, Father, but I know she keeps herself to herself. I've never met her, though. If she is anything like her mother, then make your visit a quick one and keep hold of your rosary. What with it being Halloween and all.'

Bridget Mulligan and Halloween again. 'Halloween? Is that significant, then?'

'Well, let's just say, don't go accepting a lift back to the church from her, on account of the possibility of falling off. There's only room for two. Her and her cat.'

Father John ignored the obvious hint at a broomstick, as Seamus had started asking where he was.

'You be on your way now, Father. I can manage your man. And remember what I said, will you?'

Less than ten minutes later, Father John adjusted his eyes to the dim light from an old oil lamp in Bridget Mulligan's cottage. Looking around, he felt as if he had stepped back in time.

The old flagstone floor had dips and furrows as it clung onto the sinking earth underneath. Two rush-seated chairs flanked the glowing fire, where a tall trivet supported a steaming kettle.

'Thank you for coming, Father. I'm Bridget. Take a seat, will you. Be careful; the floor is very uneven. My mother was always taking up the flagstones. Would I be getting you a cup of tea?'

Father John accepted, then regretted it, as he watched Bridget harvesting dried leaves that hung from a beam in the ceiling. Placing them in a cup, she poured boiling water from the hanging kettle. Then, eyeing Father John, she handed him the cup.

Trying to be polite, he thanked her. *Holy mother of God, do I have to drink this?*

Bridget was a well-set woman, with a quiff of curled hair that shot out from the scarf tied around her head. Her thick Aran cardigan hung over an old tweed skirt that had seen better days. This, in turn, covered the tops of what looked like the first wellington boots ever made. The dried mud that clung to them defied gravity.

Sitting down opposite him, she nodded at the cup. Father John felt obliged to take a sip.

The fire shone on her weathered cheeks, as her large green eyes smiled at a large black cat that appeared from nowhere, jumping onto her lap. 'My cat, Luz.' Bridget stroked its head. 'He turned up a year ago today. He told me his owner had abandoned him, on account that he didn't like heights.'

Staring at the dark mess from the wilted leaves at the bottom of his cup, Father John didn't reply. But he did wonder what heights the cat didn't like. Then the penny dropped. *Am I imagining things, or did she say the cat told her it didn't like heights?*

'Drink it, Father. The leaves won't poison you. I chose them to help with your indigestion.'

Surprised that she knew he was suffering, he was just about to ask what made her think that was the case, when she interrupted, 'Just common sense, through observation, Father. What else?'

'What else indeed, Bridget? Now tell me, what did you want to see me about?'

The next morning when Seamus awoke in his own bed, the previous evening's encounter with the devil was the first thing on his mind.

Getting up, he immediately rummaged through an old tin box until he found his pledge-not-to-drink badge. Pinning it firmly onto his jacket, he headed to the church.

Father John was surprised to see him so early. Before he could ask him how he was feeling, Seamus spoke. 'You were right, Father, the devil nearly got me last night. I saw him as close as we are now, staring at me with his burning eyes. He knew it was me. Called out my name, so he did. "Seamus, is that you?", he said.'

Father John was about to explain about the pumpkin lantern, but then decided against it. Making the sign of the cross for the little white lie he was about to tell, he turned to Seamus. 'I told you what would happen, Seamus. The devil's always waiting for the weak willed. You were lucky this time, so you were.'

'I'll never drink again, Father. Look.' Seamus pointed proudly to his pledge badge. 'This badge will be with me in the future. Every time I look at it, I'll remember my lucky escape. You might never have seen me again. All I have to do now is find some work to keep me out of harm's way.'

'I'm proud of you, Seamus. You're absolved from your penance. Just say one Hail Mary, and you'll be a new man. Then come round to the presbytery tomorrow. I think I can help you with finding work.'

Back at the presbytery, Kathleen was making more pumpkin soup. Father John peered into the bubbling pot. *Well, at least I know where to go to cure my indigestion next time I have to drink this.*

Crossing his fingers behind his back, he said, 'More pumpkin soup. That's nice, Kathleen. Now, tell me, when is the next Catholic Women's League meeting? I have a new guest speaker for you. Tell them to bring their broomsticks. And,' he started to laugh, 'not to forget their rosaries.'

Before he was to be challenged with another bowl of pumpkin soup, Father John light-heartedly strolled over to the church for a chat with the man upstairs.

As usual, the church was a haven of peace. Everything in its place, safe and secure from the sometimes upside-down world.

'Well, Boss,' he began, 'you did it again. Seamus Murphy's

all but cured, and Bridget Mulligan is having the last laugh, especially on me. What with Halloween, a cat named Luz, and muddy boots that made it look as if she'd been out burying the dead.

'She thanked me for not listening to gossip. Saying that her cottage was the perfect backdrop for village tittle-tattle, on account of the state it's in. She's a trained herbalist, and when her mammy died, she decided to come back to Pucklorglin and start her own business growing medicinal plants. She told me that getting the land ready for planting didn't give her much time to socialise, giving reign to village gossip. The cat is really called Willow, by the way.'

Father John got up and lit a candle as he continued. 'And that's not all. She's starting a natural healing centre. Now wait for the best bit. Did I know someone, she asked, who could do work on the cottage. Of course, *you* already know my reply, Lord. Seamus is the man. So, you see, as always, we have a win-win ending.'

Starting to make the sign of the cross, Father John stopped himself. 'One other thing that Bridget mentioned. She said her mother was married three times, so she was, and none of her husbands was Bridget's father. When I asked if she knew her father, she just shook her head, saying he disappeared one day, and was never seen again. Apparently she lived with an aunt in Dublin after that, who didn't approve of Bridget's mother's constant stream of new boyfriends or husbands.

'But now here's an odd thing, Lord. Each one of her mammy's husbands also just up and left, and never a word from any of them. The strangest thing of all, Bridget said, was that they all left on Halloween night. That was enough to get the gossip going. Amen.'

Father John made sure everything in the church was secure. Doors locked, back and front, lights off. *Of course she was trying to even out the floor.*

FATHER JOHN LOVES CHRISTMAS

'Christmas is only a few weeks away, Kathleen, and there's still no sign of the new priest for Rosebeigh parish. Sure, I'm getting painfully tired toing and froing to say Mass, plus Holy Communion, and hearing confessions. At this rate, I'll never get my Christmas sermon for midnight Mass started, never mind finish it.'

'It's a burden to bear, Father. Especially, as you say, at this time of the year. If I can do anything to help, just ask.'

'Thank you. You're a brick, so you are. I could do with some help with the nativity figures. They are in urgent need of a tidy up, to say the least. The three kings have no gifts, the baby Jesus has a missing toe, and I wish I could get my hands on the wise crack from the village who painted teeth on the ox and the ass, making them look like ventriloquist dummies. He wouldn't have time to sleep with the penance I would give him.'

'I'll get some gold chocolate money from Mary's shop for one of the kings. That will be a start. We'll talk about it when you get back from Jerry Keogh's. He's expecting you this morning, or have you forgot?'

'Not at all. But what can I say to cheer him up, that's the thing?'

Father John sat stony faced in Jerry Keogh's kitchen. Together they stared at the empty dog basket.

'The visions and voices started after Doorstep disappeared,' said Jerry. 'I love that dog, Father, and it was a good Catholic, even if it did water the church pillars from time to time. It was in a kind of offering.' Jerry's bloodshot eyes filled with tears.

'Well, it's lucky for me that the other parishioners just pass the plate at Mass in way of an offering. Now listen to me, Jerry. Firstly, have faith, and we will find the dog.' Father John placed a reassuring palm over Jerry's hand. 'Kathleen has half the village looking for it. Secondly, the visions and voices only started when you took to the bottle again. Leave off the drink, and they will leave you alone, man. The visions and voices are all in your mind. You're imagining them.'

'As God is my witness, I only drink to drown my sorrows. It's a penance, not a pleasure.'

Father John raised his eyebrows. 'Is that so, now? Well, try saying a decade of the rosary instead, and remember the visions are only in your mind.'

'All in my mind, Father,' repeated Jerry slowly. 'I'll drink to that.'

By the time Father John returned to the presbytery, Kathleen was eager to know how Jerry was holding up.

'Not good, Kathleen. Those visions of his are getting worse, and now he says he's hearing voices as well. If that dog doesn't turn up soon, he'll drink himself to death. Where in the name of God has it got to?'

'It must be nearby,' said Kathleen, puzzled. 'Sure, nobody

would steal a dog with the looks of that one. You can't even make out if it's coming or going. And to add to things, Jerry's behaviour has tongues wagging.'

Father John sighed. 'Gossip is the last thing Jerry needs at a time like this. And me being so busy with Rosebeigh parish.'

'You can leave the gossips to me, Father, and the dog finding to the Catholic Women's League. You just concentrate on your own interference.'

'What would I do without you, Kathleen? That dog was the saviour of Jerry Keogh. We'll be needing a miracle to find it.'

'Sure, we have had miracles before, Father, isn't that so?'

'Never a truer word spoken, Kathleen. And speaking of miracles, I'll be off to the church for a chat to the man upstairs.'

Kneeling at the altar, he waited for his silent thoughts to be born. While in the shadows, the bulbs in Saint Patrick's halo momentarily flicked on and off, reminding him of his narrow escape from the Wild West at the Boyles' christening. Kathleen was right, miracles can happen, you just need that little bit of faith to turn things round.

The comforting peace of the church allowed him to put things into perspective. Focusing on the donkey and the ox, he thought he saw their lips moving.

'Hello, are you there, Father?' they seemed to say.

The soft click of the church door jolted him back to reality.

'Father, is that you?' whispered a voice.

'It is, so. Who else?'

'It's only me, Father. Jimmy Boyle.'

'Jaysus, you gave me a fright. I thought.' He pointed towards the nativity scene. 'Never mind, what do you want?'

'I hear you're having trouble looking after Rosebeigh parish as well as Pucklorglin.'

'Is that so, now? Aren't you a mine of information.'

'I am that all right, Father. I have to be now that I'm working for an American company. They want everything done the day before you know what day it is. If you get my drift. And I have a solution for yourself.'

Father John wondered what the eejit had in mind, as not even the Americans could stop Christmas.

'And what miracle of the new age would that be then?'

'A portable confessional. It's all the rage in America. They're like the booths where you get your passport photo taken. The difference being, when you press the red button in the portable confessional, a video of yourself in the confessional appears on the screen, asking how long it's been since your last confession. Just like the real thing, only you won't be there. Then, when they've finished confessing, they press the blue button, and a recording of you tells them to say three Hail Marys and a Glory Be is played.'

'Let me get this straight. God's representative on Earth is to be replaced by a photo booth? Am I to be like the cherries in a slot machine; get three matching pictures and they're absolved? And, while this is going on, tell me, where in God's name am I?'

'Taking confession in Rosebeigh. You can't be in two places

at once now, can you?'

Before Father John could answer, Jimmy Boyle said he would add some lights around the crib and throw in an illuminated star at no extra cost.

'What have you got to lose, Father? The booths are very holy looking, with pictures of the Sacred Heart of Jesus, and electrical candles. And, for a small extra cost, you can have plug-in room fresheners that smell of incense. You're happy and your sinners are happy; not that there's much sin in Pucklorglin.'

'What have I got to lose, you say? Well, when Bishop Kelly hears about it, my parish for a start. *And,* with Bishop Kelly, money doesn't grow on trees—not even Christmas ones.'

'I've already spoken to the bishop. He's happy to give it a try, as he saw them himself in America. Best of all, it won't cost you a penny for ages. You get a sixty-day trial period.'

Father John knew he was tired because the idea was beginning to sound feasible, and the additions to the crib were well needed. The only problem was, could he trust Jimmy Boyle himself, after the Wyatt Earp fiasco? So, although he wanted to say no, he said yes.

'You won't regret it, Father. I'll have it all finished by the end of the week. You can relax, your troubles are over.'

True to his word, Jimmy Boyle delivered the booth on time. He'd also made sure the new Christmas lights framed the nativity scene, and the illuminated star shone brightly over the crib. The "Truth

Booth", as the villagers called it, was a great success. The queues went three times around the outside of the church, not to mention the inside, which was full to bursting with people pretending to say their rosary, but were, in reality, trying to hear what was confessed in the booth.

Flynn, to the annoyance of the waiting queue, kept appearing from the booth to ask his wife Hannah for change, and which buttons he had to press to get through to Father John.

While Jerry Keogh just couldn't cope at all. "Father, Father", he had kept asking, "Are you real, or am I imagining it, and you're not there at all?"

'Pucklorglin must be free of sin at this rate, Kathleen. My faith in the booth has gone up a notch, and my Christmas sermon is well on the way.'

'I must say, Father, the confessional booth working with all these new-fangled webs in the world, and their likes, are remarkable.'

Father John raised his eyes at her description of the confessional booth. 'You're a caution, to be sure, Kathleen, in your understanding of technology.'

'Oh, improving every day, Father. I'll soon be able to record things on the television at this rate.'

'Talking of improving every day, how is Jerry holding out?'

'He's up and down, Father. Mrs O'Shea was cleaning the brass in the church and helped Jerry light a candle for the dog. She asked him why he wanted to light a candle for it, as the dog wasn't dead yet. And Jerry said he knew that, but it would be one day. Then Flynn told him he thought he saw the dog running across the road, before admitting that he could have mistaken it for a cat, as he didn't have his glasses on. Not that he wears glasses anyway, Father, but he meant well. Tomorrow the children are going to look in the woods again, so let's pray they have better luck this time.'

'Mrs O'Shea helped him light a candle? If the dog is ever found, he'll want me to baptise it.'

'I'm wondering how much miracle time we have left in finding the dog now, Father?'

'As much as it takes, Kathleen.'

Christmas Eve arrived, and the church looked warm and welcoming. Large bunches of holly filled every nook, cranny, and corner of the candlelit church. Mrs O'Shea's cleaned brass sparkled out the reflection of the flickering flames, which, in turn, complemented the flickering eyelids of the inebriated congregation. Not an unusual happening after a night waiting in William O'Shea's pub for midnight Mass to begin.

The arrival of the new priest at Rosebeigh meant that, at long last, Father John could relax, and just worry about his own parish.

The church was all but full when Jerry Keogh arrived, walking down the aisle in what he thought was a straight line, until he arrived by one of the pews near the crib.

'Oh, would you look at that?' shouted Jerry, pointing to the crib. 'The donkey's talking to the ox, and the sheep are listening.'

Everybody turned to look.

'Jerry's been on the holy water again,' said Kevin Brady as his fellow congregation members chuckled. 'Mind you, he could be right about the talking, just look at the teeth on your two. What did they say, Jerry? Was it "gottle of gear?"'

Jerry swayed from side to side, remembering Father John telling him, "*It's all in your mind, there's nothing there.*"

After the laughter had died down, the choir, who were also well lubricated, sang the first carol. Then, after waiting for the fidgeting parishioners to settle, Father John began his sermon, which, he said, would be short and to the point.

'Christmas is a time of joy. Love and kindness with family and friends. Being kind to others. Giving support and repeating words of happiness to the less fortunate. Yet, the repetition of words in Pucklorglin have been cruel gossip. Repetition, repetition.' Father John repeated himself. 'Change your conversation and only repeat the good things.'

The sermon was in full flow when suddenly the lights around the crib started to fade. Father John, unaware of this, continued, 'Gossip repeats itself, exploding and hurting others.' At this point, the lights flashed vigorously, accompanied by the strong smell of burning plastic, which drifted through the church.

At first, those sitting near Jerry Keogh moved to one side, thinking he'd picked up something on the bog road. But as the smell got stronger, the illuminated star started to spit out shafts of blue light before it finally turned into an exploding Catherine Wheel. The congregation stood up, open mouthed, not at the explosion, but at the confessional booth, which had started to move slowly towards the crib.

Father John watched, listening in horror as he recognised his own voice coming from the booth, which was fast gaining momentum, and could have given lessons to a whirling dervish as it circled nearer to the nativity scene. Flashing cracks and bangs were accompanied by his never-ending voice. It felt more like November the fifth than Christmas, as each display was greeted with the *oohs* and *ahhs* of the people.

'Money couldn't buy this,' said Kevin Brady. 'It's even better than Saint Patrick's war paint.'

Father John's pre-recorded voice began sounding more akin to Donald Duck than a serious priest, as it repeated, "Three hail Marys and a glory be, three hail Marys and a glory be," so loud that it echoed around the church.

A final almighty bang, followed by a loud crack of fused lights brought the shuddering booth to a halt. However, Father John's voice, albeit slower now, was slurring on with its holy penance, sounding like a cow in labour.

Everybody stayed still and silent, waiting for another explosion. Each person trying hard to suppress their laughter, but the constant repetition of Father John's voice was too much for them, and as one, the congregation burst into a mass of hysteria. The only person not affected was Jerry Keogh, who knew that what he had witnessed had never happened at all, as it was all in his mind.

Finally, the last Amen from the booth slowly drawled to a halt. The congregation held its breath, waiting for an encore. Happily for Father John, it didn't happen. Then, in respect for him, and the final holy ending, everybody blessed themselves, before all eyes turned towards him.

'Well, I bet we saw a better performance here tonight than if we had tickets for The Abby Theatre itself.' Kevin Brady had no doubts about the comparison. 'Fine man you are now, Father John Phelan, ne Dublin, now Pucklorglin,' he said proudly.

The congregation clapped and cheered in agreement, but, for Father John, there was only one way to move on from all this praise.

'After that, what can I say to you all? Thank you for making me feel welcome since I came to Pucklorglin. Replacing Father Frank was a hard act to follow. We will always keep him in our hearts. And a Merry Christmas to you all. In the name of the Father, the Son, and the Holy Ghost, Amen. Now let's start Christmas Day with an appropriate carol, *Away in a Manger*.'

As everybody left the church, they were more inebriated than when they arrived. Only this time it was laughter driven.

The last to leave was Kathleen. 'Now, don't fret yourself about that mechanical box, Father. Look on the bright side. We have the real thing back, which is yourself, plus candles you can light. Good riddance to webs of other worlds and wide things.'

Father John nodded in agreement. 'Never was a truer word

spoken, Kathleen.'

When the church was finally empty, Father John studied the near burnt-out wreckage of the now silent portable confessional box in front of the crib. Jimmy Boyle had safely disconnected the electricity supply before making a hasty retreat. To be extra sure that the plugs in the nativity scene were now safe, Father John knelt for a closer look.

What he discovered renewed his faith in human nature. Not that it ever left him in the first place. *It wasn't Jimmy Boyle's fault. And there I was calling him all the eejits on the planet. Well, God forgive me. I'll make it up to him tomorrow. Amen.*

Christmas morning saw the church full to bursting point. Everybody was vying for a seat near the now defunct confessional box, secretly hoping for a repeat performance of the night before.

Father John stood in front of the congregation. 'Firstly, in my sermon last night at midnight Mass, I said it was better not to repeat the misdemeanours of others, as gossip is usually made up of half-truths.

'Some of you may think that because Jimmy Boyle installed the Truth Booth, as you like to call it, that it must have been his fault that it broke down. It wasn't. The truth of what happened came from the crib itself. For after you all went home, I discovered the culprits that fused the lights with their offering that could not wait. As I bent down to inspect the damage, I noticed the straw around the offending plug was damp. Then there was a sound from under the crib. I could hardly believe what I saw. Jerry Keogh's dog, Doorstep, unbeknown to us, has, over the past few days, given birth to three puppies in the stable. Three little Doorsteps to make a Christmas stairway to Jerry's heart. And, if that's not a good Christmas story, I don't know what is. Amen.'

After Christmas lunch, Father John sat in front of the fire. 'Thank you, Kathleen. That was a grand lunch, to end a grand day.'

'It was so, Father. And it's good to be back in the miracle business, so it is.'

'We never left it, Kathleen. Or should I say, it never left us. Jerry has offered me one of the puppies, by the way.'

A silence rested in the air as Father John waited for a comment on the addition of a dog in the presbytery.

'Well, it's either you or me who will have one of the puppies, Father, so perhaps it will be better that we share a dog? What do you say to that?'

'I can only say, Merry Christmas to you, Kathleen Byrne. And thank you for all you do.' Quickly getting back to the dog, he added, 'I thought a good name for it would be Monty.'

'But that's a boy's name. No, Father, we must have a girl puppy.'

'Would you like a glass of Christmas port, Kathleen, and we can discuss it?'

'That would be grand, thank you. Discuss away, Father, but

before you begin, I thought Cinders would make a nice name for the dog.'

'Cinders?'

'On account that *she* could have burnt the church down with all the straw in the stable, but instead we have had a fairy tale ending to our story.'

Smiling, Father John nodded in agreement. *Well, Lord, Cinders it is then. Amen.*

THE CHURCH HALL DISCO

Father John was in a reflective mood. He was thinking about the conversation he'd had with The Holy Father in Rome. *He seemed very concerned about space travel. He'd be even more concerned if he had to travel on the Pucklorglin bus. As for little green men, well, according to Jerry Keogh, he's always seeing them—but I suppose that's another thing altogether. And what about the enormity of the universe, and the existence of God himself? Who could blame anyone floundering for an answer to that mystery?*

A strong shaft of sunlight shot down through the top window of the church, bringing him back to the job in hand. A quick chat with the man upstairs.

'A problem shared is a problem solved, is that not so?' began Father John. 'Not that it's really a problem, you understand, Lord, just an observation. It's like this: Pucklorglin is a small village, which needs a boost in population. Since my arrival here, I have carried out more funerals than weddings, and the church diary is painfully low on baptisms. I was wondering if you had any ideas how to get the wedding bells ringing again? Perhaps a sprinkling of heavenly dust might help give it the boost it needs? Amen.'

Back in the presbytery, Father John started singing as he thought about his asking for heavenly dust. But where was it to be sprinkled? Although a lot happened in Mary Muldoon's shop, romance was not one of them. *Boy meets girl, where? Ah, I have it.*

'Kathleen,' he called, 'could you pop into the office for a minute? I have a great idea.'

'I'll be with you in a moment.'

Father John came into the kitchen to see what was keeping her. 'Kathleen, I have a great idea,' he repeated. 'What about a disco in the church hall?'

'First things first, Father. I was just talking to Lilly, our new Sunday school teacher, on the phone. She wanted to let us know that Jerry Keogh's Fly with the Bees club fitted in well with her lessons for Sunday school. They are going to use the back room, as the hall is too cold and draughty for the children. And as for a disco, in the church hall? Out of the question. We can't have anything in the church hall.'

'It will be fine for a disco. Nobody will see anything with those flashing lights.'

'No, Father. Since those roof tiles became loose, you've been able to smell the damp as soon as you walk into the place. The church hall must have work done on it before we can use it again. It was only the Girl Guides' bunting that hid the holes in the wall for Bishop Akuma's visit. It needs a lot of work doing to it, Father. Mind you,' Kathleen gave a thoughtful pause, 'it would be money well spent, though, as we could then hire it out. You would be surprised how many people want venues for gatherings, writing groups, and the like.'

Father John fell silent. All his plans seemed to be drifting away. 'There must be something we can do. What about a coat of paint on the walls?'

Kathleen shook her head. 'No, it's too far gone, Father. Also, the lino on the floor is full of holes; everyone would be tripping over each other. The place needs a thorough makeover, as they say on the television.'

'A makeover? And how much will that cost? You know I can't ask the bishop for any money. And I'm all but prayed out with the almighty.'

'We still have the jumble sale on Saturday, and more donations are arriving every day.'

'Well, unless we find the lost gold of the Irish kings in one of the boxes, it looks as though the disco is off, then.'

'Don't give up yet on your disco idea, Father. Leave me to do a list of things to be done, and we'll go from there.'

A few days later, Kathleen had the unexpected news that her brother-in-law had suddenly passed away. 'He's never had a day's illness in his life, Father. Sure, he was in perfect health.'

'I'm sorry to hear it, Kathleen. How is your sister?'

'As you know, they didn't really get on, but it's a shock all the same, especially the way of his going.'

'What did the man die from?'

'Thinking, Father.'

'Thinking?' Father John held his breath, waiting for an answer.

'One of those India thinking religions. That's what I call it, anyway. He used to sit with his eyes closed, not talking for hours. He only did it to annoy my sister.'

Mother of God. An Indian thinking religion. 'Was he meditating? If so, he was a peaceful man.'

'He could have been peeling potatoes for all I know, Father.'

Father John studied Kathleen's face. *I'm not going there.* 'Kathleen, you can't die from thinking.'

'Well, he did. He saw an advertisement in the paper, which promised that if you thought deep enough, you could make all your dreams come true. All he had to do was pay for a postal course on how to do it.'

'And did they? Did all his dreams come true?' Father John wondered what was coming next.

'Who knows? He froze to death before he found out, so he did.'

'Sacred Heart of Jaysus, Kathleen. You don't freeze to death from meditating.'

'You do if you sit cross legged in the garden on the coldest night of the year, with only your underpants to cover your decency. Not that I'm being personal about his state of dress, Father.' Kathleen continued, 'Anyway, they had a terrible job, apparently, so my sister said, in trying to uncross his legs. Now, what are we going to do about the church hall?'

After the revelation regarding your man's legs, Father John was still trying to figure out what kind of meditative state he was in when Kathleen repeated herself.

'The church hall, Father?'

'Am I mistaken, or are you talking in tongues? What has the church hall got to do with your departed brother-in-law?'

'My sister wants to hire it for the funeral tea. He had a large family, and the state of the hall, with peeling paint and rickety old chairs, not to mention the flooring, will be an embarrassment for her. It's going to be dull enough with everybody talking about her husband anyway.'

'He didn't really have a choice now, did he?'

Kathleen shrugged. 'One piece of good news—my sister is donating her husband's model collection to Saint Jude's. So, for once, Father, we won't have to go with a basket of turnips to the bishop for money.'

Turnips? 'What kind of models?'

'Cars and trains, and the like. Some are worth a penny or two. She will be glad to see the back of them. He had them displayed all over the house. And you never got to look at them.'

'What? How could you miss them if the house was full of them?' Father John waited, wondering what gem of an answer was heading his way.

'Sure, they were all in boxes. We never saw the things inside, just the picture on the box. And the boxes were in a better state than the wallpaper.'

Wallpaper? 'Is your sister sure she wants to donate them?'

'She will be glad to see the back of them. When he unpacked his case on their honeymoon at Rosebeigh, not a sign of sandals or swimming togs. His case was full of magazines for model car collectors.'

Father John was beginning to feel older as the conversation continued.

'The next morning, being just married, my poor sister got the bus home. Then, not hearing from him for two days, she went back to see if he was still alive. And do you know what that eejit said? He asked if his new magazine been delivered.'

'It's a sad business whichever way you look at it. But it was kind of your sister to think about Saint Jude's with the model collection. Which now means we can at least get an estimate for the work on the church hall. Can you give Seamus Murphy a ring and ask him to pop round to discuss the list of things to be done?'

'Already done, Father. He'll be here tomorrow.'

A few days later, the auction estimate for the model collection arrived in the post. Father John couldn't believe what, to him, children's toys were worth. Handing Kathleen the letter, he said, 'Even if we get the lower estimate, we can easily afford Seamus to do your makeover for the church hall. Then, after your sister's funeral tea, we can begin organising the disco. I'll ring your sister and thank her.'

'Oh, she won't be in. The neighbour has taken a shine to her, and they have gone out for a drive together.'

'Her neighbour? You don't mean Danny O'Hay, by any chance?'

'The very same, Father.'

'Sure, he's nearly old enough to be her father.'

'You have a point, but he's a fine man. Very tall for his height, with a fine head of hair and a good set of teeth.'

'I know the teeth well, Kathleen. I've seen them in a glass by his bed, on a visit. And isn't it a bit soon to be dallying with a fella. Her husband's not long passed.'

'Good luck to her, Father. She never dallied with that husband of hers. God rest his soul.'

'Getting back to the good news, Kathleen. We can tell Seamus he can start work on the church hall. Let me have the list of things that need doing and I'll go over it with him. At this rate, we'll be up and running in no time.'

'I can start work on the church hall anytime, Father.' Seamus studied the list. 'As you know, I'm also modernising Bridget Mulligan's cottage. But it's being done in fits and starts while I'm waiting for building materials and the like. Thanks for suggesting me, by the way. I must say, she's a grand girl, and we get along fine. Apart from the lack of a good cup of tea, that is.'

She's a grand girl! That's the first sprinkling of heavenly dust. 'Bring her along to the disco, Seamus. It will be a grand evening. I'm expecting a good crowd. There will be posters everywhere.'

'This is a grand idea, Father, just what the village needs. Now, what colour do you want the walls?'

'Better ask Kathleen that one.'

'What about sanding the floor? It's always good to have a slide on the dance floor.'

'You'll have to ask Kathleen about that technicality.'

'When do you want me to start?'

'Kathleen will tell you.'

'Buying tickets?'

'Speak to Kathleen.'

'Well, *you* seem on top of everything, Father. I'll start in a couple of days. What time suits you?'

'What time? Now *that* you had better ask Kathleen. If I give a time, she will say it's inconvenient, as she is always busy. What at, God only knows.' Father John raised his eyes to heaven in confused wonderment at all she said she had to do.

The renovations in the church hall were admired by all. The newly-sanded floor set off the new tables and chairs. There were modern blinds at the windows and an up-to-date tea and coffee machine. The last one having met its end from all the use on the African bishop's visit.

Kathleen said that her sister would be well pleased at the finished result.

The sandwiches and cakes were put on the new china, in preparation for the funeral tea. To give it a finished look, flowers adorned the tables and window ledges.

'Thank you, Kathleen.' Her sister gave her a kiss on the cheek. 'The cakes and sandwiches look delicious. But, I bet his family will have something to complain about. Can you believe it! They have hardly spoken to me since he passed on, especially his sister. All she said was, "how could you let him sit in the cold in his underpants?" The nerve of that one. I said, "how could I have stopped him?"'

The smell of mothballs, from the rarely-used black suits, preceded the bereaved family as they filed into the church hall. Kathleen welcomed them as they swarmed around the buffet like a flock of crows. When they finally came up for air, the plates on the table were virtually empty.

Father John wove his way through the family, listening to all their tales of woe. The only comment regarding the deceased was in relation to his collection. 'At least he had his model cars and trains,' they had said. 'He would have been half a man without them.' Saying this, their eyes rested on Kathleen's sister.

'Holy mother of God, what a miserable day that was yesterday, Father.'

'Well, it was a funeral, Kathleen.'

'That's as maybe, but when I depart this world, I want a Humerist funeral to send me off. I want everybody to have a good laugh.'

'Humerist funeral? You mean Humanist.'

'That's right, Father, and don't you forget it.'

'Have you spoken to your sister since the funeral?'

'I have; she said that his family is always like that. Apart from on Christmas Day when they are worse. She's coming to the disco, by the way. And Mary Muldoon wants another book of tickets to sell. I must say, Father, this disco idea was a marvel. Saint Jude's will have a healthy budget after this.'

'It wasn't just my idea you know, Kathleen. I had help as usual.' *Silent contemplation, coupled with a chat to the man upstairs. And you don't have to sit in the cold in your underpants to get results. God rest his soul.*

Saturday night is disco night in Pucklorglin, the leaflets that had been handed around the village proudly proclaimed.

When the much-anticipated evening arrived, first through the door was Jerry Keogh. Father John had to look twice. *Holy mother of God, he's put on a clean shirt. And Lilly, the new Sunday school teacher, is with him. They're arm in arm!*

'Good evening, Father. You know Lilly.' Jerry blushed.

'Hello, Father. I've just come from our new family.'

'New family? You're ahead of me, Lilly.'

'Doorstep's puppies. When they're ready, I'm going to have one of them.'

'And it couldn't have a better owner,' said Jerry, whose face flushed a little redder. 'Lilly has offered to help out this evening while I'm on the door selling tickets.'

'Thank you, Lilly.' Father John beamed. 'Have a word with

Kathleen. She will be glad of an extra pair of hands.'

Kathleen soon had Lilly in charge of light refreshments, while herself and Mrs O'Shea served beers and soft drinks.

Jimmy Boyle had supplied the lighting that flashed in tune with the music, and one of Jimmy's brothers, who was a disc jockey in Dublin, had offered to DJ gratis for the evening. Father John was over the moon. His instinct was to rush over to the church and give thanks, but he hadn't finished the job in hand—and he wanted to see who might be getting a sprinkling of heavenly dust first.

Standing behind Jerry, Father John kept a keen eye on the people as they filed in. Pucklorglin, Middle Pucklorglin, and Little Pucklorglin. *If it carries on like this, I will have a full wedding diary for Saint Jude's.*

'Have we sold many more tickets, Jerry? The hall is near to bursting with people,' Father John shouted over the music.

'Quite a few, Father.' Jerry rattled the tin. 'I've never been to a disco before. The noise is terrible.'

'That's what discos are all about.'

Jerry put his fingers into his ears. 'I can't hear you, Father.'

Father John didn't reply. He was looking in amazement at Seamus Murphy and Bridget Mulligan, who had just arrived together. *My God, those two scrub up nicely. I hardly recognised them. And, holy mother of God, Seamus is holding her hand. Could this be a sign of confetti in the church porch, I wonder?*

Then Kathleen's sister, accompanied by her neighbour, arrived.

'Good evening, Father. You've met Danny,' she said shyly. 'He's been a brick, so he has, keeping me company.'

Keeping her company? Right. Raising his voice over the music, 'Hello, Danny, how's your health?' *Better to be forewarned.*

Acknowledging Father John, he smiled, giving a thumbs up.

Yes, the same teeth.

As the evening danced on, Father John's mental tally sheet looked promising, so he took himself off for a chat with the man upstairs. Making his way over to the church, he was surprised how full of life he was.

First, he lit two candles—one for Kathleen's sister's departed husband, and the other just for the joy of seeing its flame dancing with the shadows in the dark.

Kneeling in front of the altar, he closed his eyes, letting the silence wrap around him. Blessing himself, he thanked the man upstairs for helping him with the idea for a disco.

'The young ones are loving it. Me? I'm happy watching them have a good time. And wait for it, the heavenly dust? I think we will have a season of spring weddings. I'll know soon enough when the tongues start wagging in Mary's shop.

'I still can't get over Jerry Keogh. I never thought I would see the day, what with the drink and all. Arm in arm for all to see. And what a nice girl Lilly is. That was a turn up for the books. Could we have a winner there, by any chance? Then to cap it all, Seamus and Bridget Mulligan are actually holding hands. Isn't it amazing how things turn out, with just a little bit of faith? One more thing before I go. Doorstep's puppy will soon be arriving at the presbytery. We definitely will *not* be needing any heavenly dust where she is concerned. So thank you, and no thank you. Amen.'

Heading back to the disco, Father John stopped and looked at the flashing lights coming from the church hall. *What a turn up for the books this has been. The interest in the hall since it had its makeover is looking very promising. As for the disco? Well, that speaks for itself. Mind you,* Father John looked up at the sky. *Who needs disco lights when you have the stars?*

THE END

Printed in Great Britain
by Amazon